Kirklees

Culture & Leisure Servic~
Re~ ~ol~~ Lane

D1586871

WHAT THE HEART WANTS

Alistair is looking for a very particular kind of wife: a country girl who would be happy to settle down to life on his farm in the small town of Shonasbrae. Bonnie, fresh from the city to open her first of many beauty salons, isn't looking for a husband and she certainly isn't accustomed to country life. With such conflicting goals, Alistair and Bonnie couldn't be less compatible. But romance doesn't always make sense, and incompatible as the two are, they don't seem to be able to stay apart . . .

SUZANNE ROSS JONES

◆

WHAT THE HEART WANTS

Complete and Unabridged

LINFORD
Leicester

First published in Great Britain in 2019

First Linford Edition
published 2020

A catalogue record for this book is available
from the British Library.

ISBN 978–1–4448–4520–4

Published by
Ulverscroft Limited
Anstey, Leicestershire

Set by Words & Graphics Ltd.
Anstey, Leicestershire
Printed and bound in Great Britain by
T. J. International Ltd., Padstow, Cornwall

This book is printed on acid-free paper

Alistair's List

Alistair winced under his sister's piercing blue gaze. He wished now he'd had the good sense to refuse her summons back to the farmhouse this lunchtime. Ailsa was as irritated as he'd ever seen her.

'So you're saying no?' She tapped her foot impatiently on the stone kitchen floor, waiting for his reply.

Despite everything, he wanted to laugh. Even as a child, she'd never taken well to not getting her own way. Age had not mellowed her.

Taking a deep breath and summoning near superhuman effort, he managed to keep a straight face — which was just as well as he didn't want to annoy her even further.

'Yes. I'm saying no.'

'Even though I've used my lunch break to drive out here to ask you in person?'

'It's still no. Nobody asked you to give up your lunch break. I could just as easily have refused over the phone.'

'I thought it would be more polite to ask in person — even though I didn't have time to take a break at all. We're rushed off our feet as always. My colleagues are having to cover while I take back some time off in lieu to come to speak to you.'

The nurse's uniform gave weight to the fact that she had indeed been busy at work. She would be going back to the hospital at any moment. All Alistair had to do was hold his nerve until that happened.

'I was hoping to get this sorted out quickly. I really don't have time to try to persuade you.'

'I don't have time, either. I have fences to mend and I can't believe you've dragged me all the way back from the top field to ask me such a daft question.'

And it was daft. Who in their right might would want to take a woman they had never met before to their own ex-girlfriend's wedding?

'Gilly's nice. You'll like her.' Ailsa was giving it one last go.

'Still no. Sorry.'

He had met most of Ailsa's friends before, but Gilly had only moved to the nearby town of Sheldonmill a matter of months ago and Ailsa did most of her socialising there these days, rather than in the quieter nightspots of Shonasbrae, so they had never met.

He suppressed a chuckle. There were no nightspots in Shonasbrae. Even the solitary pub was shut by half past nine most nights, though that suited him fine. He had to be up early for the farm in any case.

'She says she won't go without a man on her arm.'

He frowned.

'That sounds a bit pathetic.'

'Don't be unkind, Alistair. It doesn't suit you.'

'I'm not being unkind. I just don't understand how anybody would refuse

3

to attend a wedding simply because they didn't have a partner.'

Ailsa sighed.

'As I've already explained, Gilly moved up from Edinburgh to be with her fiancé. Only he suddenly decided he wasn't ready for marriage. She's heart-broken, and this wedding will be the first time she'll see him since they broke it off. She doesn't want to face him alone.'

Alistair frowned. Obviously he felt very sorry for Gilly, but what Ailsa was suggesting sounded like a terrible idea.

'She won't be alone,' Alistair pointed out reasonably. 'You'll be there.'

'Don't be difficult. You know what I mean.'

He shook his head.

'It's still a no from me.' He wondered how many more times he was going to have to say it before his sister took no for an answer.

'But you'll be there anyway. What's the harm in joining us?'

4

He shook his head.

'I'm not going to the wedding.'

'Why not?' Ailsa was frowning again. She did a lot of that these days. 'I know you and Daisy went out once or twice, but that wasn't anything serious, was it? And she must want you to be there, or she wouldn't have invited you.'

Alistair's glance moved to the mantelpiece in the farmhouse kitchen, to where the invitation was propped up behind the clock.

'No, it wasn't serious between me and Daisy,' he confirmed, 'and, before you ask, no, I'm not upset that she's marrying someone else.'

'Then why won't you help, Alistair? Why?'

So, so many reasons. And every argument Ailsa offered gave him yet more concerns. Accompanying a heart-broken woman to a wedding her own ex-fiancé would be attending sounded like he would be asking for trouble.

But it boiled down to the fact that up

until now, Alistair's romantic life had been a disaster and he was determined to change that.

'I've decided I'm getting married myself.'

If he hadn't been so serious about it, he would have laughed at the look of shock on his sister's face.

'I didn't even know you were seeing anyone.'

'I'm not.'

'Then who . . . ?'

'I haven't met her yet. He sat back and savoured the shock he'd caused. It wasn't often he managed to surprise anyone, let alone his sister.

'I've made a list of what I need in a wife. I'm not dating anyone in future who doesn't exactly match every point on it — and a woman who is so hung up on her ex that she won't go to someone's wedding alone isn't remotely who I have in mind.'

Ailsa's eyes narrowed and she pulled out a chair and sat at the scrubbed wooden table.

Alistair recognised his error immediately — he shouldn't have revealed his secret.

He had planned to keep it quiet — at least until he'd had a chance to get his own thoughts straight. But his twin sister always seemed to be able to get him to spill the beans, even when she wasn't aware he was hiding anything.

He shifted uncomfortably.

'Tea?' He diverted his attention to concentrate on making them both a drink. Maybe if he didn't say anything else, she'd let the subject go. Maybe, if he didn't look into her eyes, she would forget what he'd said.

'You've written a list?' she asked coldly. 'Of attributes you're looking for in a girlfriend?' She stared at him for a moment. He squirmed some more.

'Not just a girlfriend. A wife. I've written a list of things I would like in a wife.' He hoped the distinction would make a difference.

He wasn't taking this lightly — he was seriously looking for a life partner

— someone to share the rest of his days with. Surely Ailsa would see how important it was that he found the right person?

'A list?' she repeated, as though the meaning might suddenly change if she said the words often enough.

He brought the mugs over to the table and sat down, loosening the neckline of his polo shirt as he did so.

'What's wrong with that?' Immediately on the defensive, he hoped throwing a question back at Ailsa would calm the situation. It was obvious she thought his idea was terrible but he really didn't see what the problem was.

'What's wrong with that?' she repeated, her voice at least an octave higher than her normal tone. 'I'll tell you what's wrong with that. Getting married should be about love and romance, not a shopping list of qualities and requirements.'

'Love and romance hasn't served this family very well until now, has it?'

He watched as she winced. He hadn't

meant to upset her, but it was a fact.

'We're thirty,' he reminded her gently, 'and both still unmarried. I want children while I'm still young enough to kick a football with them — and I'd prefer to have a wife before that happened.'

Ailsa sighed.

'But, Alistair — a list?'

He shrugged.

'It's as good a method as any.'

'And what are you going to do with this list? Take out an advert and publish it in next week's 'Sheldonmill Press'?'

'I haven't decided yet. I only wrote it up last night.' Which was true. Another lonely night in his family-size farmhouse had convinced him. He needed a wife.

It wasn't that he was hopeless with women. He was well able to hold a conversation and easily managed to arrange dates but the women he'd been out with in the past hadn't been a good match for him.

Very soon into the dating process,

their differing life goals had come between them. They had all, to a woman, been keen to move away from Shonasbrae. And he had been equally eager to stay.

The next time he dated, he would make sure he and the woman concerned were compatible. He needed to meet a woman with the same ambitions as himself — someone who would be happy to settle down and be a mother and a farmer's wife.

'You might as well just try a dating agency — or internet dating.'

Her tone was cynical. Ailsa was a romantic. If he hadn't known that already, her words today would have proved it beyond doubt. She wouldn't understand that, to him, compatibility rated high above falling in love.

He knew that if he met the right woman, they would make each other happy. Love didn't even come into it.

It all boiled down to logic.

'Maybe I will.' She might have hit on something there. Now that she had brought the idea up, Alistair realised he wasn't averse to bringing in an agency. He could give them his list — they could do all the hard work for him and weed out the women who were immediately incompatible.

'And how do you know Gilly won't be perfect for you?'

'Educated guess.' He knew his sister's friends — they were all party people, just like her. Besides, if this Gilly had newly broken off an engagement and was still upset by the thought of seeing her ex-fiancé, chances were she wouldn't be in the market for rushing into another serious relationship any time soon.

'Let me see this list,' Ailsa demanded, reaching out an impatient hand.

Alistair grimaced. She'd always been bossy. His first instinct was to say no, but what harm could it do? And maybe she might know someone from the fringes of her acquaintances who would be suitable.

He got up and took a scrap of paper

from the top dresser drawer and handed it over.

She was silent for a moment as she regarded the handwritten details of Alistair's requirements.

'Young and strong?' she commented at last. 'That seems very cold and calculated.'

'She needs to be young. I want children,' he reminded her. 'Someone to pass the farm on to and to play football with.'

She gave a brief and very obviously reluctant nod.

'I suppose that's fair enough.'

'And she needs to be strong, so she can help on the farm.'

'You have farm workers for that. Surely if you met the perfect woman you could work around the fact that she didn't want to spend her days in wellies?'

'That's just the thing. I haven't met the perfect woman. That's why I'm going to try things a bit differently from now on. In future, if a woman doesn't tick every item on that list, I won't be asking her out.'

Ailsa's blue eyes were unflinching as her disapproval transmitted to him across the scrubbed wooden table.

'And what if she asks you?'

'What?'

'It's the twenty-first century, Alistair. What if a woman asks you out?'

He smiled. That hadn't happened in the entire 30 years he'd been alive so far, so it wasn't a scenario he ever expected to happen. Nonetheless, the question had been asked, so it needed to be answered.

'If someone does ask and she doesn't fall in with my list then I'll be saying no.'

Ailsa shook her head.

'So let's get this straight. Your requirements in this mythical wife are,' she picked up a pen and jabbed at each item as she read, 'young and strong; willing and able to give up whatever career she might have to work on the farm; not afraid of mud or hard work.

You want her to be good-looking, but not obsessed with her appearance — and a good cook.'

Alistair nodded enthusiastically as Ailsa read out that item. He liked his food and, even though he could fend for himself, it would be nice to have a wife who could cook, too.

She jabbed at the list again as she continued to read.

'She needs to be a country girl, born and bred, and,' Ailsa frowned, 'she has to like football.'

'Women like football.'

'Some do, it's true. But I can't believe that you'd totally disregard a potential partner if she didn't. I don't know, Alistair, I really don't think this is a good idea.'

'Well it's just as well that it's my business and none of yours.'

Offended, he took his list back and folded it carefully before getting up from the table and going to the dresser, where he placed it in the top drawer.

'What do you think Mum would say about this?'

He shrugged.

'Mum's not here, so we don't need to worry about it.'

'It's just as well,' Ailsa said disapprovingly. 'She wouldn't like it. And neither would Dad.'

'Yeah, well, it's only an idea,' he said, wishing again that he hadn't said anything about his plan. He didn't want to fall out with his sister over this.

Ailsa sighed.

'I need to get back to work,' she said. 'My break is nearly over.' She got to her feet and he went to fetch her jacket.

She sighed as she took it from him, signalling her own wish to keep things on an even keel between them by standing on tiptoe to peck his cheek goodbye.

'Just keep it like that,' she said. 'An idea. I don't want you to be hurt, and this is a recipe for disaster.'

'Don't worry about me. I can look

out for myself.' He followed her to the door.

'And you have me to look out for you, too,' she said. 'No matter who you end up marrying, you'll always be my little brother and I'll always want what's best for you.'

A little brother who was only five minutes younger and a good foot taller certainly didn't need anyone looking out for him. But it was good to know she cared.

'I just don't want you to think that this list will be the answer to everything,' she said as she opened the door to the farmyard. 'You'll still have to find this woman. She's not just going to turn up at your front door.'

'I know that, I'm not daft. But at least if I have an idea what I need in a wife, then I'm not going to be wasting any more time on relationships that will never get off the ground. Knowing we're compatible will give me a reason to stick to the plan and to make the relationship work.'

She sighed as she reached the door, then turned to look at him.

'So, it's a definite no for coming to Daisy's wedding?' The hopeful gleam in her eye let him know she hadn't quite given up yet.

But he had made his mind up. He followed her to the door.

''Fraid so.'

He was waiting for his perfect woman. Nothing less would do.

Disasters

Bonnie pressed her foot hard on the accelerator, willing her car to move this time. The engine revved as she turned the steering wheel this way and that, tyres spinning, mud splattering everywhere.

No matter what she did, her car remained resolutely stuck.

Typical. This had so not been her day. She had already been running late. Booked for a pre-wedding make-up appointment, she had been held up when a delivery had appeared unexpectedly as she was about to leave the salon, and she'd had to wait for it to be unloaded.

That had been her first mistake. Accepting a delivery that was more than a week late when she had places to be.

Her second had been relying on her

satnav, instead of looking at a good old-fashioned map. That particular error had resulted in a missed turn in the road but, in her defence, she had been in a hurry by then and there hadn't been time to look at a map.

The third and final mistake, the one that had left her so spectacularly stuck in the mud at the side of this narrow country lane, had been the one where she had decided the verge looked firm enough to drive on to as she negotiated a three-point turn so she would be able to retrace her tracks.

Now she was not only lost, but stuck, too. And there was no signal for her mobile, so she wasn't even able to call for help, or to ring her client to let her know why she had been held up.

With a sigh, Bonnie turned off the engine. She might be a city girl through to her bones, but even she knew that continuing to try this method of escape would only dig her in deeper.

She would have to walk to see if she

could find help at the nearest house. Even though her heels weren't made for hiking, she was confident she could make it as far as the farmhouse she had passed only a few minutes ago.

Hopefully someone would be in and be willing to let her to use their phone — or maybe her own phone would spring miraculously to life by then.

That was one of the many things she still wasn't used to in Shonasbrae, the way the mobile signal was so patchy around here.

Bonnie wasn't even entirely sure who she would call. Being new to the area, she didn't have contacts at a local garage.

Hopefully the farm people would know of someone with a tow-truck. If not, maybe they would have Wi-Fi and she would be able to look up a local company.

She swung open the car door and looked gingerly at the mud outside. Why had she thought it would be a good idea to move to the country?

Right now she couldn't think of a single reason.

The neat black skirt of the suit she had settled on for her uniform was too tight to even attempt a leap from the car to the road, though she suspected she would have fallen short even with the right clothing. She liked to keep fit, but athletics had never been one of her strengths and the expanse across the mud lake looked like quite a distance.

Taking a deep breath, Bonnie hitched up her skirt and stepped out of the car.

As the heels of her new shoes sank in and cold mud oozed over the top and on to her feet, she could think of a number of reasons why her move to Shonasbrae had been a very bad idea indeed.

So far, her dream of the perfect life had turned into one disaster after another. The salon she had taken over had a dwindling clientele who were suspicious of this incomer.

The flat above the salon was damp and needed a million and one things done to it. And now, just when she was trying to expand her business and had been given this chance to do a bride's make-up . . . Mud.

Lots of mud at that.

With a deep breath, Bonnie stepped from the uncertain ground on the verge, and on to the safety of the narrow road.

Maybe she would put her salon back on to the market when she got back. Maybe she would find someone as daft as she was herself, who would buy into the idea of a new start and a dream where they would make people beautiful for a living.

Maybe her old boss would take her back to the salon where she had trained in the city. And maybe her flatmate wouldn't have rented her room out yet, and she might be able to move back to the home she had left.

Trying to ignore the mud oozing from her shoes, Bonnie set off along the road — leaving a trail of muddy footsteps in her wake.

She had known, of course, that the flat above the salon would need work — and that she would need to be patient with the locals. She had been warned that relationships were forged slowly in this neck of the woods. She hadn't expected things to be quite this difficult, though.

She was quickly running out of money, her small inheritance from her grandfather already hugely eaten into when she had bought the salon. Unless she found some new customers fast, she would soon have no choice but to return to the city.

Lifting her chin, she marched along the road, her determination becoming stronger with each step she took.

The salon would be a success even if it killed her. Bonnie didn't do failure. She had been a high achiever all her life — and she had big plans for her business.

Hairdos of Shonasbrae was to be the first of many salons she was planning. She didn't intend to rest until her name was known across the country.

Right now, she would have traded potential fame for some comfortable walking shoes. If her shoes had been unsuitable for mud, they were definitely not built for the uneven road surface. She wondered if the local council ever came out this far for repairs.

With a deep breath, she tried not to squirm as her feet slid this way and that inside what had once been a smart pair of shoes.

It was taking much longer than she had expected to reach the farmhouse. She had seriously misjudged the distance. It wasn't even as though anyone drove past who might have offered her a lift. These roads were quiet.

It wasn't only the distance she had misjudged — she could have sworn this hill wasn't so steep when she had driven down it . . .

Stopping for a well needed breather, she quickly checked her mobile. She was still firmly out of circulation.

'Useless thing,' she muttered, as she

pushed it back into her jacket pocket.

At the exact point when she had just about given up hope of ever finding it, she rounded a bend in the road, and there it was — the farmhouse that all her hopes were pinned on.

'Thank goodness,' she muttered as she walked in through the gate — knowing enough about country life to close it carefully behind her — and made her way on to the farmyard.

She knew nothing about farmyards, but this one seemed quite ordinary — though, with the exception of a handful of hens, it was deserted.

As she approached the house, a couple came out.

He was tall and broad shouldered, wearing jeans and a black polo shirt, his arms bare despite the chill in the air. She was smaller and dressed in what looked suspiciously like a nurse's navy blue uniform, under a zipped up navy jacket. They each had dark brown hair.

They glanced at her in obvious surprise as she approached.

'Hello,' the man said, more in shock than in greeting.

Bonnie guessed they didn't get many visitors if this reaction was anything to go by. She couldn't say she was surprised, as they were so out of the way — miles from anywhere. Poor things.

How Bonnie would hate to live out here. The small town she had foolishly moved to was bad enough. You couldn't even get a cup of coffee after five in the afternoon.

And as for late-night grocery shopping, forget it. The night-life left much to be desired, too — no smart restaurants or clubs, and only one rather depressing pub.

Bonnie was used to bright lights and city hours. She liked clubbing with her friends, going out to smart bars — and dancing. That was the one thing that upset her most about Shonasbrae — there was nowhere to dance.

Still, she could live with it while she got her salon up and running. And then she would be off, leaving it in the hands of an as yet unappointed manager, while she looked for the next addition to her empire.

'Hi.' Bonnie offered a half-smile as she wondered how she could bring up the subject of the very large favour she wanted.

'You seem to like mud,' the woman said, smiling as she pointedly glanced down at Bonnie's shoes.

Bonnie smiled awkwardly.

'Maybe it would be more correct to say that mud seems to like me.'

'Tell me, what do you think of football?'

'Ailsa, stop it.' The man frowned, and the woman's smile widened.

Bonnie got the impression she had walked in on some private joke that she didn't understand.

Suddenly uncomfortable, she wished she had waited in the car. Someone would have driven by eventually. Waiting it out, however long it took, would be preferable to this feeling of being completely out of her depth.

'You want to know what I think about football?'

'Yes,' the woman confirmed. 'Football. Do you like it?'

'Watching it or playing it?'

'Either.' The woman's tone was clipped. She and the man looked at Bonnie expectantly.

'Well, if you must know, I hate it. I hate the noise, I hate the crowds. And I can't see any point in watching anyone chasing after a ball on a dirty field when they could all just exercise quietly in a nice, clean gym.'

'That's disappointing,' the woman said as she arched an eyebrow and grinned.

The man was still frowning. Bonnie felt her face grow warm. She didn't know what she had said wrong, but she was pretty sure they were laughing at her — or at least the woman was. The man, if his expression was anything to go by, was just in a very bad mood.

If Bonnie hadn't been desperate for assistance, she would have marched straight out of there but escape was a luxury not open to her. She needed to persuade these two very strange strangers to help, so she could get out of here as quickly as her mud-encrusted heels would allow.

'My car's stuck in the mud down the lane,' she said quickly, waving vaguely in the direction of her car. She wanted to ask why they had been so interested in her views on football, but she ignored the urge. That wasn't important. Getting her car back on the road was. 'And my mobile isn't getting a signal.'

'The mobile signal is a bit patchy around here,' the man said.

'I wondered if I could possibly use your phone to call for help, please?'

'You don't need to use the phone.' The woman began to walk to her car. 'Alistair will help you,' she said. 'He and his tractor have pulled people out of the mud a number of times. I'll have to dash, I'm afraid, and leave you in his capable hands.'

Alistair. So this man's name was Alistair. It suited him, Bonnie decided, belatedly thinking she should probably have introduced herself as soon as she'd landed in their farmyard.

'My sister — Ailsa,' Alistair told Bonnie as the woman drove off. 'She's needed back on the ward.'

'I see.' Bonnie nodded, not really knowing if this was any of her business. 'And was . . . er . . . Ailsa . . . was she right? Would you be able to help me get my car out of the mud, please?' She hated to ask, hated to think she might be indebted to this big, rather grumpy man, but what choice did she have?

Quite unexpectedly he grinned and Bonnie had to make a concerted effort to concentrate. He wasn't that bad looking when he was smiling.

In fact, he was rather handsome, she was startled to discover. She had imagined all farmers would be ruddy faced and overweight. But this one definitely wasn't — even if he was rather grumpy.

'Yes, I can pull your car out of the mud. I'll give you a lift down there in the tractor.'

Now that was an offer she would dearly have loved to refuse but, realistically, what other choice was there? She was already getting blisters where her unsuitable shoes had rubbed the backs of her heels on the trek up here. She would only humiliate herself if she tried to limp back.

'Thank you,' she said, her tone subdued as she contemplated the ride ahead. Tractors didn't look terribly safe, in her opinion — and they definitely weren't elegant. She smiled in an effort to seem gracious.

'And I wonder if I could use your phone anyway to make a quick call. I was on the way to see a client and I got lost. I need to let her know I'm on my way.'

He gave a short nod.

'This way,' he said.

Bonnie slipped her shoes off at the door. She might have had a disastrous day, but her manners were still sharp enough to realise that traipsing mud into the home of a new acquaintance — particularly one who was trying to help her — was probably not good form.

Then she followed him indoors.

Bonnie's Knight
in Shining Armour

Alistair wasn't very happy with his sister. He knew she'd thought his plan for a list had been daft, but she hadn't needed to laugh at him so openly. He also knew Ailsa had been trying to make some sort of point about this woman here turning up on the doorstep — which had been totally uncalled for and had left their unexpected guest obviously embarrassed.

In effort to make amends, he smiled.

She smiled back. Even so, things were getting awkward.

'Like Ailsa said, I'm Alistair,' he supplied, realising it would be easier to be on first name terms rather than thinking of her as 'this woman', even if he didn't intend the acquaintance to last long.

Pretty though she undoubtedly was, despite Ailsa's pointed remarks, he could tell at a glance that she fell far short of his requirements for a wife. Those mud-caked shoes, and her visible distaste for the state they were in when Ailsa had pointed them out, told him all he needed to know.

Not to mention the very smart-looking outfit — a skirt no less — and the glossy hair that fell just below her jawline. None of it screamed 'farmer's wife' at him. And from now on, just as he had told Ailsa, the type that did suggest 'farmer's wife' was the only type he was interested in.

'Bonnie,' she said, holding her hand out.

He took her hand and her handshake made him think again. Her grip was surprisingly firm, her skin surprisingly rough for someone who otherwise looked as though she hadn't been near a day's work in her life.

His interest was piqued. Maybe he had misjudged her. Maybe she had hidden depths. And, despite what he had told Ailsa, the football alone wouldn't be a deal breaker . . .

'Phone's over there.' He nodded towards the dresser. The same dresser where his precious 'wife list' resided in the top drawer.

'Thanks.' She went over in her stockinged feet. Without the heels she was tiny — completely the opposite of the healthy farm-helping partner he had in mind for a wife.

That train of thought had to be stopped right now. He knew nothing about her. Even if she had ticked every single one of his requirements, she might already be spoken for.

He tried not to listen as she spoke to her client. Really he should go into another room and offer her some privacy. But he found himself held spellbound as her melodic voice offered apologies and explanations. Something about hair, he gathered, and make-up.

He stifled a smile. She was from another world. A world he wanted no part in — which was why he had written down that any prospective wife should not be self-obsessed with her looks.

It seemed all was well with her client as she was smiling as she put the phone down.

'She said not to worry. It's only a practice run and, as long as I'm there on time for the main event, she's willing to forgive me for being delayed this time. Country girls are so much more laid back than city clients.'

'Not always.' He was thinking of Ailsa. She was pretty high-maintenance and hated to be kept waiting. 'What is it you do, exactly?'

Why had he asked that? He had already established he wasn't interest in whatever it was she did. But he supposed it was only polite to make idle chat as they went back outside to where the tractor was parked behind the farmhouse.

'I'm a hairdresser and beautician,' she said. 'I've just taken over the salon on the high street in town. Been there three months now.'

'And how's it going?'

She frowned as she slipped her feet into her still muddy shoes.

'Not brilliant, if I'm honest. The regular clients seem to have abandoned me and I'm not having much luck finding new ones.'

She stopped talking now that the tractor was in view.

Alistair smiled when he saw her look of horror. Not unkindly — but city types were given to that sort of reaction sometimes when faced with the realities of farm life.

He'd seen it before in the faces of the guests who had holidayed here. Never before when faced with a tractor, admittedly, but some of them were shocked by the harshness of the work he considered quite normal.

'Why don't I walk back to the car?' she suggested. 'I can give you directions for where to find it and meet you down there. It won't take me long to catch you up.'

He glanced pointedly at her unsuitable shoes.

'However quickly you walk, it will take too long,' he told her pointedly. 'I only came back for my lunch — I need to be back in the top field. There are workers waiting for instructions about what to do with my new fence.'

She took another look at the tractor, then obviously realising she was in no position to lay down rules, she nodded.

'You don't need to look so worried. I know it looks pretty fierce, but you won't need to cling on to the outside. It does have a passenger seat.'

Her face softened into something of a smile, and he decided not to tell her that the passenger seat in question was normally reserved for the dog — the same dog who would be sitting there now if she hadn't decided to stay out in the field with his farmhands.

He guessed Bonnie wouldn't care to be told about that — not when she was wearing such a smart black skirt. One that would not be improved by the addition of animal hair.

Alistair climbed into the cab with the ease of one who had done so a million times before. Then, realising she would find climbing even a few steps a difficult manoeuvre, especially given her attire, he reached down on a whim, grabbed her hand, and helped her into the cab.

She took a deep breath as he started the engine and the tractor roared into life.

'Today's client is new,' she explained.

He got the feeling she was trying to take her own mind off a tractor ride she obviously wasn't enjoying. 'She's getting married in a fortnight, and I'm doing a practice run of hair and make-up for the bride and two bridesmaids.'

He nodded.

'That will be Daisy's wedding you're talking about.'

'That's right. Do you know her? Am I far from her place?'

Did he know Daisy? Daisy was one of

the reasons he had compiled his list. She was one of the many women who had seemed so compatible on a first date, but who had bored him senseless with their nonsense talk of clothes and pop stars after five minutes of chat.

She was a nice enough girl, just not Alistair's type — just as he hadn't been hers.

Daisy had met an accountant shortly after she and Alistair had parted ways, and within six months she was engaged to him.

'Her parents own the big house along the main road,' he told Bonnie as her car came into view. He smiled as she waved a frantic hand so that he wouldn't miss it. 'You just took a turning too soon. You're about five minutes away once we've got you back on the road.'

'Thank goodness.' She smiled the first genuine smile he had seen from her since she had been faced with the tractor.

He found himself smiling back.

They had her car out of the mud in a jiffy.

'Thank you so much for this,' she called through her open window. 'I do men's hair in the salon, too. Call down any time and I'll give you a free cut to say thank you.'

As Alistair stared after her, he raked a hand through his hair. He hadn't been aware it needed a cut, but now Bonnie had mentioned it, perhaps it was getting a bit long. Maybe he would pop down — even if the thought of going to a women's salon would have had him running for the hills even an hour ago.

★   ★   ★

She had meant to be kind and had made the offer in good faith to say thank you to him for pulling her car out of the mud, but when she glanced in her rear-view mirror and saw the look on his face she realised she had most probably caused grave offence — the last thing she wanted to do.

Blast.

This was supposed to be a new start and alienating people wasn't part of her business plan.

Besides, there had been nothing wrong with his hair. It had been lovely, in fact. A bit long, maybe, but it suited him. She would have to apologise.

Bonnie gave one last look in her mirror and saw that he had already climbed back into his tractor.

She should maybe come back this way later and say sorry. For now, she had a client to see and to convince that she was the right beautician for the job.

A Job Well Done

Daisy was lovely — natural beauty. Tall and elegant with the kind of luminous skin and long shiny hair that most women would kill for. She also seemed to be a very nice person, if her concern for Bonnie was anything to go by.

'How awful for you, getting stuck in the mud.' She stood aside to let Bonnie in. Bonnie faltered and glanced down at her mud-caked feet.

'And don't worry about those shoes,' Daisy told her with a smile. 'Dry mud will sweep up in no time.'

Bonnie couldn't leave muddy footsteps — not even dried muddy ones — in someone else's house so, just as she had at Alistair and Ailsa's farmhouse, she slipped her shoes off on the doorstep and stepped inside.

'How did you manage to get the car out?' Daisy asked. 'I know from experience that you don't drive out of that kind of situation easily.'

'I walked back to the farm I'd just passed, and the farmer helped. He said he knows you. His name's Alistair.'

Daisy's smile widened.

'Oh, Alistair's such a lovely guy. I'm not surprised he helped.'

Bonnie wanted to ask so much more about the mysterious farmer, but knew it wouldn't do, to start gossiping. She was here to do a job and she had already blotted her professional copy book by arriving both late and covered in mud.

She followed Daisy into the living-room of her parents' house, and found two other women sitting with glasses of wine.

'Can I get you one?' Daisy asked.

'No, thank you. I'm driving.'

'Of course. A cold drink then? Or a cup of tea?'

Bonnie didn't want to be a bother, but her adventure had made her thirsty and, if she was going to do her very best with the bridal hair and make-up, it would probably be a good idea to rehydrate.

'A cup of tea would be fab, thank you.'

While Daisy went to fetch the drink, Bonnie smiled at the other two women.

'I'm Lucy and this is Emma,' the one closest to her said. 'We're Daisy's brides-maids. Did you have far to come?'

For the second time that day, Bonnie found herself relaying the story of how she had just moved to the small town in the valley and had taken over the hair and beauty salon.

She stopped short of letting them into the secret about her lack of trade. If they realised that customers were thin on the ground, they might report back to Daisy and they would all wonder if there was something wrong with the place. Or with her.

There wasn't, of course. Both the salon and Bonnie were fine. They just needed to attract new customers and build trust.

'Oh, yes.' Daisy admired herself in the mirror as Bonnie put the finishing touches to the bridal look that had been requested. 'This is splendid. If you can repeat the same on my wedding day, I'll be very pleased. You've made me look like a much better, more glamorous version of me.'

Bonnie smiled, pleased with the reaction.

'It helps if the canvas is good,' she said truthfully, referring to her client's clear skin and symmetrical features and thick glossy hair. Daisy's smile shone in response.

'Now . . . ' Bonnie looked at the two bridesmaids. 'Who's next?'

Lucy and Emma were equally delighted with their results — which boded well for Bonnie's new business. She had heard word of mouth was the best form of advertising, and she hoped this lot would do enough chatting to their other friends to at least bring a few customers in.

'Now,' she said, as she packed up her

brushes and sponges and opened a different box, 'would anyone like their nails painted? To make up for me keeping you waiting so long earlier?'

Once she was finished here, she would pop by the farmhouse on her way home. It would be the least she could do. Even if he and his sister had seemed to be laughing at her when she'd first turned up in their farmyard, Alistair had been kind. And he had left his own work to help her out of a fix.

In her book, her apology for insulting his hair needed to be made swiftly. When she was wrong, Bonnie always owned up and she liked to put things right as soon as possible.

The bride and bridesmaids eagerly offered their nails for painting, and for the next hour Bonnie continued to do what she did best — talk to customers about hair, make-up, and clothes.

She knew some people — namely her family — thought her interests were frivolous. But she knew how important those things were. The right look could make someone feel a million dollars and could be worth more than even a session with the most accomplished therapist for someone at a low ebb.

Bonnie prided herself on giving the best service, listening carefully to her clients' wishes, and on making those wishes come true. She loved her job. She loved the power she had to make people feel good about themselves.

'I'll be here bright and early the Saturday after next,' she promised as she left. She knew the way now, so shouldn't get lost again.

⋆ ⋆ ⋆

It didn't take her long to drive to Alistair and Ailsa's farmhouse.

There was a bit of a fuss going on in the yard. A well-turned-out family — mother, father and three noisy children — were loading suitcases into the back of their big, shiny car.

'Hello,' Bonnie called cheerfully, walking towards them. 'Is Alistair around?'

They stopped their chatter and turned to looked at her blankly. Then the woman seemed to catch on.

'Oh, you mean the farmer chap.'

'Yes, I suppose I do.'

'No idea where he is,' the man said. 'I thought he might have been here to see us off, but seemingly not.'

'To be honest,' the woman added, 'we've barely seen anything of him all week. I'll be glad to get back to civilisation, to where people know what customer service is.'

With that, they got into their car, slammed the doors shut, and drove off — leaving Bonnie to stare after them in the now deserted farmyard. She was left with the distinct impression that she had been well and truly told off — and she had no idea why.

'What was all that about?' she asked the hens who were clucking about the yard.

Despite the mystery family's assurances that he wasn't around, she went to the door anyway, and knocked.

The disappointment when he didn't answer surprised her, but she put it down to the fact she had been ready and willing to apologise for any offence she had caused.

The wind had rather been taken out of her sails by her knight in shining armour not being at home.

She would have to work up the courage for another apology some other time.

With a sigh, Bonnie headed back to her car. Maybe he would turn up for that haircut, you never knew. In which case she could make it clear to him then that she hadn't meant to insult him.

Two's Company

'Come on, Jess, let's go home.' Alistair and the collie were the last out on the field as the sun was sinking below the horizon.

They were nearly finished with the fence, and they should be able to put the sheep back in here by tomorrow.

Knowing there would possibly be food involved at the other end of their journey, Jess pushed in front of him and climbed into the tractor first — taking the seat that Bonnie had sat in earlier.

Alistair smiled. He, too, was looking forward to his dinner, but that was pretty normal after a hard day out in the fields. He was planning to eat, then he'd take a quick look at his accounts, before an early night.

He knew he'd be asleep just as soon

as his head touched the pillow — before getting up early tomorrow to start it all over again.

That was as exciting as it got for Alistair.

He grinned.

He loved his life and, with any luck, his plans and the hard work he was putting in would ensure that the farm would be secure for generations to come.

Farming was a tough business these days. Even with diversification, sadly there were no guarantees.

'We have a great time, don't we, Jess?' he said to the dog. He glanced across and Jess was staring across at him, devoted as always. He just wished again he had someone to share all of this with — the farm, the lifestyle, a family . . . a human someone.

He imagined for a moment what it might be like to have a wife waiting for him. Someone to sit with in the evenings, to talk over his day, to ask her about hers.

His list had started almost as a joke. But the more he had written, the more he had realised that he was being serious.

He really did want to find a wife, someone who would complement his way of life and who would be happy to share his dream and to work alongside him to turn it into reality.

He had seen first-hand what happened when someone wasn't suited to the lifestyle. He shuddered, steering the tractor out of the field and on to the road.

That was why he was adamant that he would only marry when he had found the perfect candidate. However long it took.

'It's a good life, Jess,' he told the dog. 'We just have to find someone with the imagination to see that.'

Judging by his luck so far, it was likely to take a lot longer than he had hoped.

Take that woman from earlier, for example — Bonnie — he could no more imagine her living here at the farm than he could imagine her on the moon.

Her face as she had climbed on to the tractor ... she screamed city girl through and through, from the tips of her highly unsuitable shoes to the top of her glossy hairdo. That kind of hair would last five minutes on a day out in the fields.

He grinned as he remembered how she'd had the cheek to suggest his hair needed a cut. At least his hair was functional for a farmer — it kept his head warm in the winter and protected it from the sun in summer — and that was about all he required of it.

He blinked as he drove the tractor into the farmyard. He must be more tired than he had imagined because it looked as though Bonnie's car — complete with mud splatters from its adventure earlier today — was parked there.

What was more, it looked as though

Bonnie, now changed into clean shoes, was getting out of her car, a box in her hands.

Jess gave a loud bark as she saw their visitor.

By the time Alistair had parked the tractor at the side of the farmhouse, the Bonnie apparition had walked around to meet him. And it seemed she was very real, after all.

Jess raced off to circle around her, giving a suspicious bark every now and then — trying to work out if she was friend or foe.

'Hello, there.' Bonnie arranged the box in one hand and held out the one she had freed up. Jess hesitantly approached, gave a sniff, then signified with a wagging tail that, as far as she was concerned, Bonnie was OK. Not that it meant as much as it should have done. Jess liked everyone.

Bonnie smiled, then turned to Alistair.

'Hi,' she said, holding aloft the flimsy white box. 'I've brought cake. To say thank you for pulling my car out of the mud earlier.'

'Did you make the cake yourself?' That was rude — even to his own ears. But it was important for him to know. Though why he was trying to make her conform to his good cook requirement when he had already established she was unsuitable in every other way was anyone's guess.

She shook her head, leaving floundering the glimmer of inexplicable hope he'd harboured that she might at least match one item on the list.

Why did he feel so flat about it? He didn't even know her. He hadn't even realised she existed until this afternoon. And she had cemented, with her every word and deed since they had met, the many reasons why she wasn't suitable.

Alistair knew he had no time to waste. He was knocking on. His chances of the family he so wanted to crown the life he had built for himself here was diminishing at every turn.

But he still found himself wishing he

could get to know her better — even if she was completely unsuitable as a farmer's wife.

'It's shop bought.' She smiled, exhibiting not even a slight embarrassment about revealing that fact, which made him realise just how little they really had in common. In the circles he moved in, shop-bought cake was something of an embarrassment. If he was bringing cake to anyone's house, he would have made sure he had baked it himself.

Not that he would dream of telling her that, of course. Even he wasn't quite that devoid of good manners.

'I thought you were going to cut my hair to say thank you.'

At that point, oddly, she did seem a little embarrassed. He frowned as her cheeks began to glow a soft shade of pink. Making her uncomfortable hadn't been his intention.

'You didn't seem too keen on that suggestion and I wondered if I'd maybe been a little rude.'

Yes, she had been, but Alistair wasn't the type to hold a grudge.

'If I accept the cake, does that mean I don't get the haircut?'

She smiled.

'No. You can have both if you want. The least I can do. I don't know what I would have done without your help today. I'd have lost an important new client, that's for sure.'

'It was nothing. Five minutes of my time.' His fingers brushed against hers as he took the cake from her and, quite unexpectedly, his hand tingled in response. 'Want to come in and help me demolish it?'

★ ★ ★

There was nothing wrong with her appetite, even if she hadn't baked the cake herself. She had agreed to share his supper as well as the cake, and he smiled as she tucked into the stew he'd put in the slow cooker earlier.

It was nice to have company. And

having dinner with Bonnie was much more fun than going over the accounts — even if he would have to make up for lost time after she'd gone. He had big plans to develop the business he had built here, and he had a meeting arranged for early in the week to go over those in detail with his accountant.

For now, though, he was going to enjoy this meal and his guest's company.

She enjoyed the food much like a farmer's wife would, rather than the way he imagined one of those looks-obsessed city girls would pick at their food.

He was glad about that. He had no time for picky eaters. Food was meant to be eaten and enjoyed. And a meal for two, he reflected, enjoyed by both parties, was much more fun than eating alone.

The Business Plan

Bonnie wasn't quite sure how she had ended up eating her dinner with this handsome farmer whom she had only just met, but she was happier about it than she should have been.

The whole set up, with the cosy farmhouse and the dog sleeping under the table as they ate, seemed so right.

'I hope I'm not putting you out,' she said belatedly as she finished the last morsel on her plate. She hadn't meant to stay long when she had accepted his invitation. She had only meant to pop in for a cup of tea and a slice of cake.

Actually, she hadn't even expected any kind of invitation when she arrived — she had planned to leave the cake and go. But then he had offered to share, and once in the kitchen, he had mentioned dinner and asked if she would like to stay for that, too — and the aroma of the stew had made her mouth water . . .

'Not at all.' He smiled easily and she got the impression that she really wasn't outstaying her welcome. 'Would you like seconds? Or are you ready for that cup of tea and slice of cake?'

'Seconds? How many people were you catering for?'

He laughed.

'I always make a big pot and freeze portions for another day.'

'So I haven't eaten Ailsa's share?' She maybe should have checked about that before tucking in — it was a bit late now to be worrying about that. 'That's a relief.'

'Ailsa doesn't live here. She was only visiting earlier.'

'So you live here with . . . ?' She knew she was overstepping the boundaries of polite conversation. She had only just met the man, for heaven's sake, but there was something about him that made her curious.

'On my own.'

'Awfully big place for one.' Be quiet Bonnie, she silently urged, but now she had started, she seemed unable to stop. She knew from her chat with Daisy earlier that he was unmarried, but that didn't mean there wasn't a romantic interest on the scene.

For some reason, it was suddenly important to her to find out — even though it was none of her business.

'There is just me, for the moment.' He gathered the plates and took them over to the large sink that stood underneath the kitchen window.

'Cake?' he asked over his shoulder, as he went to fetch some plates.

'Yes, please.' Thankfully, her curious tongue took the hint and stopped talking about his private life. It wasn't as though he was the kind of man she would be interested in romantically in any case.

She frowned as that thought crossed her mind.

In tact, there was no type of man she should be interested in, if she were honest. She had made a promise to herself when she moved to Shonasbrae that her business would come first.

Romance would have to wait until her salon was a success. And, in fact, until the next salon was a success, too. And maybe the one after that, as well . . .

Though the way things were progressing, it was going to be a very long wait.

'You said earlier that things weren't too good with the salon?' He seemed to read her thoughts and didn't mince his words as he brought the cake over to the table. Now it seemed it was his turn to be inappropriately curious.

'I did,' she confirmed. 'I'm only hoping business will pick up.'

'How was your meeting with Daisy?'

'Fine.' She picked up her fork and attacked the cake. 'She's nice. So are her friends.'

'I'm glad you got on with them. I've been thinking about your salon since you told me about it earlier.'

She felt her eyes widen. The last thing she had expected was for this farmer to have her beauty salon on his mind.

'Have you?'

'What you need is to create a buzz around town. And women like Daisy — and possibly Ailsa — will be the key.'

Bonnie thought about Alistair's sister. When they'd met earlier, she had seemed detached and haughty. Bonnie couldn't imagine her wanting to get involved in any kind of marketing initiative for someone else's salon.

'I don't mean to be rude, but what do you know about running a salon?'

Thankfully he didn't seem in the least offended by her question. He leaned a little closer, his brown eyes bright with the excitement of a good idea.

'It's a business, isn't it? And I've been running this place single-handed since I was eighteen.'

She was loath to break it to him, but she couldn't help herself.

'I'm pretty sure running a farm is a little different to running a beauty salon,' she persisted and instantly winced as she realised how rude that must sound.

'A business is a business,' he told her, seemingly not offended in the slightest. 'I've turned this place around,' he told her eagerly. 'It's not just a farm any longer.'

'Really?'

He nodded.

'Don't get me wrong, the farm is still important and the animals will always come first, but I also have a holiday business here, a few chalets in the woods that I rent out.

'And while we might not cut hair here, we do have to attract new customers and keep the existing ones happy.'

Suddenly the mystery family from earlier made sense. She told him what they'd said.

'They didn't seem terribly happy when they left.'

He shrugged.

'City types,' he said. 'They just don't get it. The whole point of this place is that guests are left to entertain themselves in peace and quiet.'

'Aren't you worried they probably won't come back?'

'Can't please everyone. And I wouldn't want to try. Most of our visitors don't want to be fussed over. That's our unique selling point — visitors aren't pandered to.'

Bonnie smiled. She could see he wouldn't want to fuss over guests. He wasn't the type.

'Maybe you need to advertise that fact so you don't attract the wrong types.'

He smiled and his gaze met hers, and just for a moment her breath caught and time seemed to pause.

'Perhaps.'

'How do you manage that along with the farm work?'

'It helps that I don't sleep much.' He grinned. 'But I also have people who work for me. On the farm I have a couple of guys from the village, and with the holiday business I have people who clean the cabins and I employ an agency that deals with the publicity and web presence.'

It seemed he had all bases covered in the running of the farm and the holiday business, so maybe he did know what he was talking about after all.

Bonnie decided to be quietly impressed.

She had thought that Alistair was a set-in-his-ways farmer — not that there was anything wrong with that. But now it seemed that he had hidden depths — dynamism and ambition.

But there was something bothering her about Alistair's holiday chalets.

'I'd never have thought of Shonas-brae as a holiday destination.' What she really wanted to say was that it was the last place on earth she imagined anyone would want to stay at for a break.

There was nothing to do here, she reflected for the umpteenth time.

Nowhere to go. And for the short time she had lived here, it had rained every single day.

And the mud . . . She suppressed a shudder. There was so much of it.

He shrugged a large shoulder.

'People want different things. I appeal to those who want a quiet time — a retreat from the real world.' He grinned. 'The country can be very restful,' he said, in defensive mode, 'and the idea of a stay on a working farm appeals to a lot of holidaymakers. They like the animals, and the fresh air.'

She had never been more aware of her city-girl status in her life as she still found it difficult to imagine. Animals she liked, in theory — and fresh air, too. But she found it difficult to see how Alistair's farm could compete with the vibrancy and buzz of bright city lights.

'And are you happy to have guests here?' It struck her that anyone who would choose to live on this remote farm had to like their own company.

'Most of them are all right. Maybe I would prefer to concentrate on the animals and the land, but to be honest I had little choice. Farming isn't what is was and we're all looking for ways to make ends meet.'

She took in everything he had told her. Maybe he was qualified to offer business advice after all.

'What do you have in mind for the salon?'

'You need to identify your customer base and let them know you're there.'

She nodded. This was nothing she didn't already know, but he had been kind and helpful and she didn't want to throw his advice back in his face.

'You need to entice them, let them see what you can offer.'

She nodded — again knowing all this, and again being too polite to tell him to stop mansplaining. She knew he meant well and a part of her wanted to know where this was going because she guessed he had more ideas to share.

'Maybe,' he continued, 'you could

arrange an open afternoon, so they can see for themselves.'

She sat up a little straighter in her seat.

'That's actually not a bad idea — or it wouldn't be if I knew some people to invite.'

'You could start by putting out invitations to everyone in Shonasbrae. Tell them to bring their friends. Show them what your salon is about. Offer them drinks and food. Talk to them. I'm sure if they actually got to know you they'll be quite happy to let you loose on their hair.'

'Is that how you feel, Alistair?' she couldn't help herself from asking. 'Would you be happy to let me loose on your hair? Will you come for that free haircut I offered? You've haven't actually said that you will.'

It was suddenly important that he agreed. Because so far, even though they'd had a bit of a chat about it, he hadn't actually agreed.

'To your beauty salon?' He seemed

dubious and her heart sank. But he seemed to pick up on how much it meant to her and then he smiled. 'In or out of the salon, I can't think of anyone I would trust more with my hair.'

'That's very kind of you to say.' She felt her cheeks flush. That had to be the nicest compliment she'd had in months — if not years. 'And the open day is a great idea. But ... ' She sighed, wondering how to word this. 'I don't think it would work for me right now.'

'Why not?

He really had underestimated the depths of the mistrust for a new beautician locally — and exactly how quiet her salon had been.

She sighed. There was no choice but to be honest with him.

'I don't think anyone would come.'

He was quiet for a moment.

'Ailsa would,' he said at last, 'if I asked her.'

'Why would you do that?'

He grinned.

'Why wouldn't I?'

She smiled back.

He was, she decided for the second time that day, a nice man. As well as a very handsome one.

No Point in Wishing

Alistair wasn't quite sure himself why he'd made the offer on his sister's behalf. He wasn't even sure where the idea of an open day had come from in the first place, if he were honest.

She had been looking at him expectantly, and he had felt the need to come up with a suggestion that would help. He knew he had been rambling, talking about stuff she already knew up until then.

He only hoped his suggestion would work and that lots of potential customers would turn up — and that Ailsa would go. His sister, much as he loved her, could be unpredictable.

And she might not take well to Alistair speaking for her — or of his assertion that she would do as he asked, which was understandable.

Even as he had assured Bonnie that

Ailsa would go, he knew he should have checked with his sister before giving any guarantees.

If Ailsa did object, she would dig her sensibly shod heels in and do the opposite — because that was what his sister did.

But he didn't like the idea of Bonnie struggling to get her business off the ground. She might have worn unsuitable shoes for the country earlier today, but she had taken note of her mistake and he was impressed to see she had worn a pair of flat brogues for her visit this evening.

She deserved for her business to do well for that fact alone.

He knew it was wrong to judge a woman by her shoes, but shoes were important in the country. Besides, Bonnie's attitude had shown that she was adaptable and that impressed him.

It wasn't even just for Bonnie's sake. He loved Shonasbrae and he knew it needed incomers if it was to survive. People with ideas and enthusiasm who would keep the small town alive.

On a personal level, as he was keen to stay in the area and to raise a family here — a family he hoped that might one day take the farm over — it was important the place thrived.

With the tide of young people moving to the faster-paced cities where there were more opportunities, it was his civic duty to encourage anyone who wanted to invest in the area.

It was the civic duty of all the inhabitants of Shonasbrae — present and past. He would have to remember to repeat that to Ailsa when he was trying to persuade her to help. That was if Bonnie took up the idea, of course.

She was looking particularly dubious as she considered his suggestion.

'Well, I suppose it might work,' she said. 'I'll give it some thought.'

He gave a short nod, convinced by her tone that she was being too polite to tell him she hated the idea. Even while he was disappointed, silently he gave thanks that he would not need to explain his rash offer on Ailsa's behalf and plead with her to help after all.

He would have to give some thought as to another way he could help. He didn't want her business to fail — and he didn't want her to disappear from Shonasbrae, never to be seen again.

They had finished their tea and cake and Bonnie had stood up and was putting on her jacket when they heard the back door opening, and footsteps sounded up the passageway to the kitchen.

Jess gave a half-hearted bark, which was nothing more than a greeting and meant she must know the newcomer.

Alistair and Bonnie both looked towards the door as it crashed open, and Ailsa stood there. Her jaw dropped open as she took in the cosy scene before her — the dishes in the sink, the cake plates and tea mugs still on the table.

She very visibly reached her own conclusion in two seconds flat.

Alistair didn't often see his sister lost

for words, but Ailsa recovered quickly and a smile lit her face.

'Hello, again,' she said to Bonnie. 'Didn't expect to see you again so soon.'

Bonnie's cheeks turned a little pink.

'I came to say thank you to Alistair for pulling my car out of the mud. And to apologise for insulting his hair.'

Ailsa's head snapped around so she could glance at his hair and her eyes narrowed, but Alistair was glad she said nothing for the moment.

Still Alistair held his breath. It wouldn't be unheard of for Ailsa to tell someone in this situation that they were maybe going a little overboard turning up on the doorstep and that a simple 'thank you' at the time would have sufficed.

But maybe she read the situation and sensed his tense manner, because she only smiled and nodded.

'I'm sorry to have interrupted. I'd have waited until tomorrow if I'd realised Alistair had company, but I think I must have left my purse when I was here earlier. At least I hope I have. If I haven't, then I've lost it.'

'It's on the dresser.' Alistair nodded over to the side. 'It must have fallen out of your bag. Jess found it earlier. You're lucky I was in here at the time. She mistook it for a chew toy. You could have lost everything.'

Hearing her name, the collie got up from her bed under the table and ambled over for congratulations on her find.

'There's teeth marks on it,' Alistair added necessarily, 'but I don't think she ate any of the money.'

Ailsa smiled and bent down to pet the dog.

'Did you find my purse? You clever girl.'

Alistair's eyes met Bonnie's over the touching scene and they shared a smile.

He was aware of Ailsa's curious glance as she went to retrieve her purse.

'Well, I'll be going.' Ailsa popped the purse into her pocket. 'Leave you two to your supper.'

'No, don't go on my account,' Bonnie was too quick to say. 'I was just leaving in any case. Thank you so much for the meal, Alistair. And for the lift out of the mud earlier, too.'

'My pleasure.' Alistair found he meant it, too. It had been a delightful diversion, meeting Bonnie. Maybe she was completely unsuitable as a wife, but he still hoped they could become friends. You could never have too many friends and he had enjoyed her company. 'I'll see you out to your car.'

The evening air was cool and it was getting dark. They stopped at her car and Alistair wanted to say something — to find some excuse to see her again, even though it would be quite irrational for him to do so.

'Don't forget that offer of a haircut,' she said as she opened her car and got in. 'Ring me tomorrow and I'll book you in. Without your help I'm sure Daisy would have cancelled the booking. As it stands, I have my first major job since moving to Shonasbrae. You saved the day, Alistair.' She smiled.

Normally, Alistair took any compliment with a pinch of salt, but he was unaccountably pleased by her praise.

'Maybe we could have dinner again some time, too,' he said, then wondered if he should have said that. He didn't want her getting the wrong idea. Not when he was on the hunt for a wife. It wouldn't be helpful to acquire an unsuitable girlfriend along the way.

'I'd like that.'

He was still grinning as he went in to find his sister making fresh mugs of tea.

'I didn't mean to chase your girlfriend away.' It was almost as though Ailsa had read his thoughts.

He frowned.

'She just came to say thank you for earlier. Just like she told you.'

'If you say so. I quite fancy a slice of that cake. Is it OK if I help myself?' She cut herself a generous slice and took a bite. 'Lovely.'

'Bonnie brought it.'

Ailsa smiled, wiping a crumb from the corner of her mouth.

'Did she now?'

'To say . . . '

'Thank you,' Ailsa broke in with a laugh. 'And to apologise for insulting your hair. I'm sensing a theme here. I wonder if she would be quite so grateful or so sorry if you weren't considered to be such a catch around here.' She wrinkled her nose. 'Though I can't see what any of them see in you.'

'Thanks. Right back at you.' They laughed at the good-natured teasing, then Alistair became serious for a moment. 'In all honesty, though, if I'm such a catch, why am I still single?'

'Because you're fussy.'

He looked offended.

'That's not a bad thing,' she hurried to tell him. 'Better to make sure you're compatible with someone than rush into a disaster. We both know how disastrous an unsuitable match can be. But your list does kind of limit things a bit,' she added. 'There aren't many women around these parts who will fit the criteria.'

For the second time that day, he wished he hadn't mentioned the list to Ailsa.

And, just a little bit — as he thought of Bonnie — he kind of wished his list was a bit different. It might have worked if he was looking for someone who was brave enough to move from the city to a small, quiet town in the country and throw her all behind a business venture.

Or if he was looking for a partner who knew how to entertain over a meal for two. Or someone to cut his hair.

Sadly, none of those things were priorities.

And, even if Bonnie had met some of his requirements for a wife, he knew he might be able to rewrite his own rules and overlook those qualities that might not be quite so compatible.

But she didn't match a single one.

So there was no point in wishing.

Was there?

Unexpected Invitation

Bonnie gave a lot of thought to Alistair's suggestion as she drove back to the salon and let herself into the little flat above.

She had learned a lot from Nita, the owner of the salon where she had trained, about the business. She was confident in all aspects of hairdressing and beauty — and about running a salon day-to-day. But Nita's place had already been established when Bonnie had joined.

Hairdos of Shonasbrae had been left to run down for such a long time that Bonnie was effectively starting anew. She needed to attract a new clientele and an open day wasn't the worst idea she had ever heard in her life. It would give the locals a chance to meet her, for a start.

Cutting someone's hair, painting

their nails or waxing their legs was quite a personal thing to do. It was difficult for some women — and men — to relax in a salon environment with a complete stranger. Hopefully, Daisy would put out the word that Bonnie knew what she was doing and an open day might just nudge things along a bit.

She began to formulate a list of what she would need.

Food would be a must — some nibbles to entice prospective customers in. And bubbly, so the locals could help her to celebrate her new venture. She would need to get posters printed to advertise the event — and maybe run off some more leaflets detailing what she offered in the salon would be a good idea — especially as she was running low, having already posted most of her supply through letterboxes in the village.

Yes, she thought, as she kicked off her shoes and put the kettle on, this could work.

Besides, it would give her a reason to

call Alistair again — to see if his offer of inviting his sister and her friends along was still open.

She had enjoyed sharing a meal with him tonight. He was easy to get along with and she hoped they could be friends.

He was attractive, too, she thought, not for the first time. Though he wasn't her type. Definitely not.

Way too outdoorsy for her tastes. Bonnie didn't really do outdoors. She much preferred being inside, away from the elements that could play havoc with skin.

Besides, she wasn't in the market for romance. Nor would she be for at least another ten years. Not if she wanted to concentrate on getting her business empire off the ground.

It would be good to see him again, though. As a friend. She needed friends in Shonasbrae.

And the more she thought of her open day, the more excited she got.

Her head was buzzing with plans,

and she found it difficult to sleep. But after a restless night, she woke up early to a beautifully sunny day and for the first time she glimpsed why someone would want to live here permanently.

'Hello, beautiful town,' Bonnie mumbled to herself as she pulled back the curtains and marvelled at how a bit of sunshine transformed the view.

It seemed symbolic. She was enjoying this new perspective of her new home town just as she had determined to make a real effort to encourage new customers.

She hoped that both the sunshine and her new optimism would last.

With reluctance, she forced herself to walk away from the window and, once she was settled with a cup of coffee, she began to make proper plans — starting with calling caterers, and designing her poster.

And, while she worked, her salon remained resolutely empty. Still, at least the lack of customers meant she had time to work on her plans, she decided, as she chose to look on the bright side.

She wondered how long she should leave it before she contacted Alistair. She didn't want to bother him again so soon when she was sure he must be working hard on the farm — but equally she didn't want to leave it so long that he might forget her.

And, if she was totally honest with herself, she wanted to see him again.

Her heart gave a little flutter at the thought.

★   ★   ★

The phone was ringing in the kitchen as Alistair arrived back at the farmhouse for his morning break. His two farmhands had come back with him, eager for a hearty morning snack to stave off the hunger brought on by a good morning's work.

Alistair nearly toppled over in his haste to pull off his muddy boots before running inside to answer the phone before whoever it was rang off. He heard the men laughing as he ran along the hall.

'It'll be cold callers, lad,' Hugh called. 'It always is. No point breaking your neck to answer them. Though they'll be able to help you claim compensation, no doubt, if you do.' The older man laughed at his own cleverness.

'Don't be daft, Dad,' the younger man, Zac, said. 'Who will he claim from? Himself? It would be his own fault and this is his property.'

Hugh was probably right. It was most likely a nuisance all. Nobody ever phoned the landline these days. Most of the bookings for the cabins were made online — and his friends and family always phoned his mobile, unless he was in a bad spot for a signal, in which case they kept trying the mobile until they got through.

He had a strong feeling this wasn't a cold caller, though, and he snatched up the receiver before they could hang up.

'Hillside Farm.'

'Hello, Alistair?' a familiar feminine voice spoke.

His heart leaped as he realised his instinct had been quite right. This was very definitely not a nuisance caller.

Even though she wouldn't be able to see him, he smiled.

'Hi, Bonnie.' He struggled to sound cool in the face of the unexpected — and not to mention inexplicable — joy in his heart.

'Alistair, I've been thinking about your idea of an open day here at that salon — and I really think it might work.'

'That's good news. I'm sure it'll raise your profile in the village.'

'I wanted to ask if you still think Ailsa might come?'

All worries of explaining to Ailsa, a busy nurse, that he had offered some of her precious free time to an almost stranger were swiftly dismissed. He just wanted to help Bonnie. The minor inconvenience of having to convince

Ailsa meant very little in the face of that.

'I'm sure she'll be delighted.' His voice was so full of confidence that even he believed his own words.

'And I wondered . . . ' She paused and he heard her take a deep breath. 'I wondered if you'd come along, too. The salon is for men as well as women. And you did say you'd trust me with your hair.' She laughed softly. 'Even if you didn't quite go as far as saying you'd come to the salon.'

So she had noticed his avoidance tactic.

He knew he had sort of agreed she could cut his hair, but the truth was Alistair hadn't been into a unisex salon in his life. He went to a barber's — a manly place that was only one small step up from a spit and sawdust establishment, a glum and tiny place above a shoe shop in the centre of nearby Sheldonmill.

He'd always gone there. Ever since his mother had stopped cutting his hair when he was six years old, his father had taken him along when he'd gone to get his own hair cut. He smiled fondly as he remembered his father's instructions to the barber.

'Not too much off. My wife will be livid if he goes home with all those curls gone.'

These days, a short back and sides twice a year did him fine. In between, he let it grow.

However, as he had realised yesterday after Bonnie's comments, he was due a haircut. And since she had made the offer to cut his hair, he had to admit that he was curious about what went on in the salon. And even more curious to see her at work.

'When were you thinking?' he asked.

He heard an intake of breath down the line.

'As soon as I can arrange things.'

'You'll be in danger of nobody turning up if it's too short notice.' He was stalling for time, trying to summon the courage to say yes.

'All the more reason for you to come along with your sister.'

He laughed.

'Fair enough. Listen, do you have a pen?' he asked. 'I'll give you my mobile number. That way, when you ring me with the details, you won't have to take pot luck on catching me in next time. If I don't have a signal, just leave a voicemail and I'll pick it up as soon as I can.' He was still smiling as he put the phone down.

'So,' Hugh said thoughtfully, 'Bonnie, is it?'

'Don't look at me like that,' Alistair said as he took the cup of tea the younger farmhand, Zac, handed him. 'Thanks, Zac. Bonnie is just a friend.'

Definitely just a friend. Most emphatically nothing more.

Hugh wasn't buying it.

'If you say so.'

'She's new to the area. I'm doing what anyone in Shonasbrae would do and I'm being neighbourly. She's planning an open day at her place, so the locals can get to know her.'

Zac was grinning, too. Alistair decided it was time to teach them both a lesson.

'What do you both feel about an afternoon at a beauty salon?'

That wiped the smiled from their faces. Alistair chuckled.

'Is that an order, boss?' Hugh sounded horrified.

'It's a heartfelt request from a friend.' Alistair always tried not to get too heavy handed, having found the saying about catching more flies with sugar rather than vinegar to be true.

Besides, pulling rank over something like this wasn't exactly ethical, and Alistair always prided himself on being a decent employer. He hoped they would find it in their hearts to help out a newcomer.

'When?' Zac asked. 'When would you want us to go to this salon?'

Alistair wondered if he should have given them advanced warning at all. Judging by the expressions of woe, he wouldn't be surprised if they didn't both develop a nasty disease and phone in sick on the day.

Maybe he just wouldn't tell them what day it was. It would be a surprise when it happened. But, again, he couldn't do that to them.

'Bonnie's going to let me know,' he said, then chuckled again as he looked at their stricken faces. 'She's planning to lay on food.'

That cheered them up a lot. They were men, like himself, who liked to take care of their stomachs.

'Why didn't you say that?' Hugh asked with a hearty laugh. 'Food makes all the difference.'

Alistair smiled, hoping it was going to be just as easy to persuade a lot more people to attend.

Open Day

Just as he expected, Ailsa wasn't keen when he phoned her that evening.

'Alistair?' The incredulous tone rang in his ear. 'What do you want?' She sounded suspicious, as well she might, as he hardly ever phoned anyone. Ever.

'A favour.' He knew it was a huge cheek when he had turned down her request so recently, but this was an entirely different prospect. He wasn't asking her to give up a whole day's work or to get involved in a romantic drama involving parties that were completely unknown to him.

Or, indeed, to attend an ex-girlfriend's wedding.

Yes, this was completely different. And he had every right to ask. Anything that would help Shonasbrae regain the vitality it was in danger of losing as the youngsters moved out of town had to be a worthy cause.

Quickly he explained about Bonnie's business and the open day. Though he stopped short of telling her that he'd already assured Bonnie that his sister would attend.

That news needed to be broken gently. The request needed to be made with tact.

'If she's good at her job, then word will spread,' Ailsa insisted. 'I'm not sure an open day will serve any purpose.'

'But how will anyone know she's good at her job if they don't give her a chance?'

He could almost hear Ailsa frown.

'I suppose you have a point.'

He grinned. It wasn't often Ailsa admitted she might be wrong.

'So you'll come along to this open day?' His tone was hopeful.

'I have a hairdresser,' she reminded him. 'I've been going to her for years.'

He sighed.

'Please? Just come along and see what you think. And maybe bring a friend or two? She's new to the area. She doesn't know anyone.'

'You're taking a big interest in this hairdresser.'

He held his breath — was Ailsa going to make too much of this?

'I'm helping out a newcomer.'

'Are you sure you're telling me the truth? You really aren't interested in sussing her out as a potential wife?'

'I'm telling you the truth,' he said, though it was surprisingly difficult to form the words. 'She would be a most unsuitable wife — I managed to work that out as soon as I met her, without any sussing whatsoever.'

'If you say so.'

'I do. Now will you help out or not?'

'Oh, all right.' The agreement was grudging. 'Although if I have to go to this open day, then maybe you could consider doing a wee favour for me in return?'

He sighed. He had thought it had been a little too easy to convince her. He should have known that she had given up her argument for him to go to Daisy's wedding with Gilly a little too easily.

'I'll go to Daisy's wedding.' His tone was flat as he pre-empted her request. And his agreement was every bit as grudgingly given as hers had been.

★　★　★

Bonnie didn't know quite what she had expected when she had planned her open day, but it certainly hadn't been a salon full of farmers. Well, to be fair, there were only three of them, but they took up so much room they seemed to be a much bigger crowd.

'Thank you so much for coming,' she said, smiling at her guests. 'Please help yourself to refreshments.' She waved towards a table in the corner where the buffet had been laid out.

To be fair, she hadn't expected much of the caterers she had called in at short notice, but they had put on a mouth-watering spread.

Not waiting to be told twice, two of the farmers bolted over to the corner, looking pleased to be on familiar territory. The third wasn't so quick off the mark and lingered at her side.

'Thanks.' Alistair grinned at her. 'They'll be happy now they're being fed.'

'No, it's me who should be thanking you — for the idea and for bringing your friends.'

She didn't tell him, but she was wondering if this might not turn out to be a disaster. There had been no response at all to the flyers she had posted through people's doors yesterday.

A hundred of them, all for nothing. And she had been chased by a dog — and tripped over a loose paving stone on a unkempt pathway to someone's front door.

And there was no sign of Alistair's sister, Ailsa, which meant that Alistair had probably failed to persuade her to come.

'Ailsa will be here soon,' he said, seeming to read her mind.

She smiled, touched that he had kept his promise and asked her.

'And I hope some of the locals might turn up, too,' he added.

Maybe they would. As well as the flyers, she had called Daisy, who had said she would try to pop by with her bridesmaids.

On cue, the bell rang and Daisy came in, closely followed by her friends.

'Excuse me,' Bonnie said to Alistair, 'I have to go over and say hello.'

Before she knew it, there was barely moving room in the salon. Maybe people had seen Alistair and company enter, or perhaps followed the trail set by Daisy and friends. Whatever the reason, curious locals had taken the bait they had been offered, and they were all here for a look.

Even more surprising, though she didn't seem overly delighted to be here, Ailsa had made an appearance.

'Seems you don't need us any

longer,' Alistair said when he managed to speak to Bonnie as she circulated.

'Of course I need you.'

Well, that had sounded a little too earnest. She cringed. But Alistair didn't seem to notice. Thank goodness.

'I'd better take those two back,' he said, nodding towards Hugh and Zac. We've lots to do. Still having trouble with that top fence and we need to get back to it.'

She smiled and glanced in the direction of the two very awkward-looking men who were still hanging around the snack table.

'I can see it's not their scene.'

'No.' He laughed. 'Nor mine, either, if I'm honest. But it's been an experience.'

'It made all the difference, you know, having you here while we were waiting for everyone to turn up. I might have lost my nerve and closed early otherwise.'

Their eyes met and held, and just for a moment she found it hard to breathe.

'My pleasure,' he assured her as he held her gaze. And he really seemed sincere.

A guest jostled her in the crowd and quickly brought her out of whatever trance she was in.

'Sorry.' The possible future customer smiled and dodged out of the way.

'No problem.' Bonnie was grateful for being jolted back to reality. She turned her attention back to Alistair. 'While you're here, I'll book you in for that haircut.' She reached over to the counter and quickly flicked through the pages of her appointment diary. 'How about next Saturday morning? Nine o'clock?'

He still didn't look too sure about the arrangement and she hoped that giving him a few days to get used to the idea might make things a bit more acceptable to him.

'Aren't you supposed to be getting Daisy ready for her wedding next Saturday?'

Bonnie nodded.

'Yes, but I'm not due at the house until eleven.' Daisy wasn't getting married until two, so Bonnie didn't need to be there too early.

'I suppose it would be useful to have a haircut before the wedding,' he said thoughtfully. 'Ailsa's already been on at me to smarten up. I've not to turn up looking like a farmer.' He grinned.

Bonnie tried not to let her surprise show. As an ex-boyfriend of the bride, Alistair was the last person she expected to be on the guest list.

But then, he had said that they had only dated a couple of times. And they had been lifelong neighbours. So maybe it wasn't so odd after all.

In any case, it was none of her business, and she concentrated instead on writing Alistair's name in the book and repeating the details in a clear hand on an empty appointment card.

His hand brushed against hers as he took the card and she struggled to retain her composure.

'I'll see you then,' she said. 'Don't be late.'

'Wouldn't dream of it.'

And, with that, he gathered up his well-fed assistants, and led the way out to his Land Rover.

That was the start of it. Once she had written Alistair's name into the pages, others began to discuss the possibility of treatments and, very slowly, her appointment book began to look a bit healthier. A trim here, a pedicure there . . .

It wasn't quite a full diary, but she suddenly began to feel a bit more optimistic about the future of her business.

A Word of Warning

As everyone began to leave — curiosity about Shonasbrae's new beautician satisfied — Bonnie was aware of Alistair's sister hanging back, waiting to speak to her.

She forced away a brief flash of apprehension and painted on a smile as she stepped towards the other woman.

'Thank you so much for coming along, Ailsa. And for bringing your friends.'

Ailsa had brought a group of women with her, but was on her own now, her friends having wandered away a while back. One of them had booked in for highlights before leaving.

'No problem.' Ailsa frowned as she paced the salon. 'I can't believe Alistair was here.'

It seemed an odd thing for her to say, but Bonnie kept smiling politely, ignoring the niggling feeling that Ailsa disapproved although Ailsa hadn't actually said anything to confirm the suspicion.

'It was his idea, this open day. I'm grateful for his support.'

'How did you manage to persuade him?'

OK, this time there was no mistaking the subtle bite to the tone.

'I didn't. It was his idea,' Bonnie repeated. 'He had to persuade me.'

'No, I meant how did you persuade him to come to the salon today? It's really not his scene, as I'm sure you've gathered.'

'I did ask him if he'd come, that's true. But I didn't undertake any underhand methods to persuade him at all, it was a decision he made all by himself.'

She knew she was going on the defensive, and she was sure antagonising Alistair's sister was probably not a good idea, but Bonnie didn't like the suggestion that she had somehow duped him.

'He was keen to support the idea,' she continued, her tone a little softer. 'With it being his idea after all. And he was keen to support the salon — as I'm sure he would have been with any other business in Shonasbrae.'

Ailsa gave a short nod.

'He's always been kind.'

Bonnie waited a moment, convinced that wasn't what Ailsa had meant to say. Eventually, the other woman sighed.

'Look, I don't know if I should be saying this . . . I mean it's not really any of my business.'

'I'm a hairdresser and beautician,' Bonnie pointed out patiently. 'People confide all sorts in me. It's very unlikely you're going to be telling me anything I haven't heard before — and whatever you tell me won't go any further.'

'Well, it's just I don't know how you feel about Alistair,' she said, 'or what you think might be going on. But, well, Alistair might be giving you the wrong idea. You really aren't his type.'

Ah — so she was being warned off. It

would have been horribly rude to laugh, even if that was what she wanted to do, so Bonnie assumed an expression of utter seriousness.

'I shouldn't imagine I am,' she agreed cheerfully. 'Just as he isn't my type.'

'I don't mean to be rude,' Ailsa continued, 'but I don't want anyone getting hurt.'

'Ailsa, I don't mean to be rude, either, but really I hadn't even thought of Alistair that way. Yes, he's good-looking and yes, I like him. But romance is the last thing on my mind at the moment. I am not interested in your brother in a romantic way.'

Ailsa's eye's widened.

'You're not?'

'No,' she confirmed. 'I'm not. Besides, even if I were, Alistair and I have only known each other a matter of days. We've shared the sum total of one meal, and we've spoken for maybe a couple of hours. And neither of us has shown any romantic interest in the other. Under any circumstance you really are being premature with your warning.'

Ailsa's tense expression relaxed into a smile. Bonnie flirted with the idea of being offended that the other woman was so pleased that no romance was in the offing.

Instead, she pinned a polite smile on to her face.

'Was there anything else I can help you with?'

'Actually, yes. Can I book a pedicure? I think I need to start looking after my feet. I bought new sandals the other day for Daisy's wedding, and my toes look horrid — all hard skin and discoloured nails.'

Ailsa shuddered, and Bonnie bit back a smile. This was a problem she'd heard a million times before — and one she thankfully could help with.

'I could do it now if you have time.'

Ailsa shook her head.

'I've no time just now, but later in the week would be great.'

The appointment was made, and

Bonnie wrote out a card with the date and time and handed it to Ailsa.

'I'll look forward to seeing you,' she said, her professional smile firmly in place.

She refused to allow Ailsa to see how much this conversation had bothered her. It was daft. What she had said to the other woman about her feelings for Alistair had been 100 percent true. So why did the prospect of Alistair being nothing more than a platonic friend make her feel so flat?

'See you next week.' Ailsa gave a little wave as she went on her way.

★   ★   ★

Bonnie was left in her empty salon, wondering exactly why she wasn't Alistair's type. She might not be looking for romance, but she was pretty miffed to be told outright that she wasn't good enough for Ailsa's brother.

She allowed her smile to fade as she watched through the window as Ailsa made her way to the car she had parked outside.

The salon was quiet now, with no prospect of more customers and there had been enough excitement for one day. She was going to close up early and phone her friend Nita back home for a chat, then she was going to relax in a hot bath with a good book.

She was about to turn the sign to 'Closed' and lock the door when someone pushed it open. A woman a couple of years older than herself stepped in and looked around the now empty salon, disappointed.

'Oh, I've missed it.'

Bonnie glanced about at the debris left after the open day.

'I'm afraid so.'

'I'm Lianne,' the other woman introduced herself. 'I had been hoping to speak to you about the beauty treatments you have on offer.'

Bonnie glanced towards the nearly empty refreshments table.

'There's still some cake left.' She

smiled. Alistair's lads hadn't been as thorough as she had given them credit for. 'And I hid a bottle of wine in the back room earlier. Why don't you sit down and we can have a chat?'

★   ★   ★

'I think you need to pay us a bonus for today, Alistair,' Zac said as they took their tea break later that afternoon. 'Going with you to your girlfriend's salon isn't exactly in our job descriptions.'

'Yes — a bonus is a good idea,' his father, Hugh, added, taking a sip of his strong tea.

Alistair grinned. His workers did like to tease him.

'You got fed down there, didn't you?' he reminded them. 'The number of sandwiches alone that you ate made for a hefty bonus. Not to mention I saw Zac booked an appointment to have his hair cut.'

Zac looked a bit embarrassed about

that. As a young man, he was very particular about his appearance and had endured some good-natured teasing from his father about hair products and the like.

'What's wrong with that?' he asked defensively — and Alistair immediately felt rotten for having put the boy in that situation. Just because he and Hugh were too past-it to care about fashion and male grooming products, there was no need to pick on the lad.

'Nothing's wrong with it at all. I was just pointing out that you both got something out of it, so maybe I don't owe you a bonus.'

Hugh took a quick drink of his tea and picked up a slice of cake.

'This isn't your usual cake,' he said disapprovingly, but still took a large bite.

'No,' Hugh agreed. 'There is a fruit loaf if you'd rather.'

'So where did this one come from?'

'Bonnie,' he said. 'She brought it round the other night.' Alistair had kept the cake hidden in a tin until now, hoping to avoid exactly this conversation. But he had realised this morning that if he didn't finish it today it would probably be past its best. Just as he and Hugh seemed to be hurtling towards their own sell-by dates, he thought with a smile.

'Did she now?'

He didn't like the knowing tone of Hugh's voice as he spoke — nor the gleam of amusement in young Zac's eyes.

'Like I've said, we're friends,' Alistair insisted. 'Nothing more. So you can stop putting two and two together and getting twenty.'

Hugh laughed.

'If you say so.' But he didn't sound convinced.

'We've nothing in common. If we went out it would only end in disappointment.' Alistair's heart sank a little as again he thought of his list and how incompatible he and Bonnie were.

He had enjoyed her company when

she had joined him for dinner the other evening. She had brightened the place up. He began to think maybe Ailsa had been right. Perhaps his list had been a bad idea after all.

Engaged on the Spot!

Bonnie warmed to Lianne on sight. Tall and blonde with a ready smile, she looked as though she would be a lot of fun on a girls' night out.

Over a second glass of wine, Bonnie turned to salon's sign to 'Closed', just as she'd planned to do when Lianne had arrived, and they settled down in the comfy chairs that had been installed in a quiet corner as a waiting area.

'I had my eye on this place,' Lianne confided, taking a sip of her drink, 'but funds are a little short just now. They always are when you have a sixteen-year-old to take care of. There's always something — new trainers, new phone, new jeans . . . and none of it's cheap.'

'Boy or girl?'

'Boy,' Lianne said, picking up a generous helping of the leftover cake and attacking it with a fork. 'I suppose it could be worse,' she confided between mouthfuls. 'If he'd been a girl I'd be having to shell out for make-up, too.'

Bonnie grimaced. Having children had never featured in her life plan. Not that she actively didn't want any, but with no serious relationship to speak of, it had never been at the forefront of her ambitions.

Now, as she saw how fond Lianne was of her son, she began to think having children might not be such a bad idea, after all.

'I'm on my own with him,' Lianne confided, 'and whatever anyone tells you about being a single parent, the reality is ten times harder.'

Bonnie nodded, sympathetic, but also completely ignorant of the realities.

'I can imagine it must be very tough.'

Lianne nodded.

'Have more cake,' Bonnie offered, not really knowing how else to help. Cake always made things better, didn't it? At least it worked for her.

'Thanks.' Lianne grinned and took another slice. 'To make matters worse, I think I'm about to lose my job.'

'Oh no. What do you do?'

'Receptionist,' Lianne confided, 'for a firm of accountants in Sheldonmill. I've been there since I left school, but they've been taken over by a bigger firm, and I think they will be closing our office. We haven't been told officially yet, but the rumours are rife.'

Bonnie had been involved in similar discussions countless times. As a hairdresser, people often told her their troubles. And she tried to offer constructive advice, although very often all they really wanted to do was talk.

'Have you been putting feelers out for a new job?'

Lianne nodded.

'But to be honest, I'm not sure if I want to carry on with that line of work. It was handy when Connor was younger because it fitted in with him, but now, well, I think I maybe need a bit more. Something I might enjoy.'

'And what do you think that might be?'

Lianne's eyes lit up and she sat forward in her chair.

'I'm good with people,' she said, 'and I'm interested in beauty and fashion . . . '

Suddenly, the reason for this visit became crystal clear to Bonnie.

Lianne wasn't here to make an appointment, nor for a cosy chat — or to make a new friend for that matter. She was looking for a new job.

'I'm not really looking to take on any employees just yet.' Bonnie was loath to admit that the level of business she had picked up didn't warrant a member of staff — not when she was keen to portray herself as successful. But she also hated to let Lianne think there might be the chance of a job here.

'Maybe one day, but I'm not busy enough just yet,' she finally admitted quietly.

Lianne took her chance.

'I know all the women in town,' she said. 'I could increase trade so you were rushed off your feet ever hour of every day . . . if that's what you wanted.'

Of course that was what Bonnie wanted, but did she want the responsibility of an employee . . . someone who would be limited to being on reception?

If she were to take anyone else on they would need to be able to pitch in and help with all aspects of the business.

'I'm willing to retrain,' Lianne said, as though reading Bonnie's mind. 'I'm at a stage in my life where I'm looking for something I'll enjoy — a job that I can be passionate about instead of just something to earn a living by.

'I've heard my current company will be generous with redundancy, so if you were willing to take me on as an apprentice, I could take a pay cut until I could prove to you that I'm worth a full salary.'

She was a good salesperson. The fact

that Bonnie was considering this pitch Lianne had made for a job that didn't actually exist proved that fact beyond doubt.

'When would you be available to start?' Bonnie asked.

'I've heard they're going to speak to us next Monday morning. That's why I'd like to have a plan in place as soon as possible. I don't like uncertainty.'

'A trial run,' Bonnie decided. 'I could offer you a job, on a trial basis, just to see how things work out.'

The words had barely fallen from Bonnie's lips before Lianne launched herself from her chair and enveloped Bonnie in a big hug.

'Thank you so much! You won't regret this. I promise.'

Winded by the suddenness of Lianne's grateful hug, there wasn't much Bonnie could do, other than to marvel that this had to be the least professional job interview she had ever been involved in.

And she'd still employed the inter-viewee. Maybe she wasn't cut out for being an employer, despite all her plans and dreams.

But Lianne was a warm and bubbly person, obviously just right for working in what Bonnie hoped would soon be a busy salon.

Lianne left as quickly as she had arrived, and Bonnie stared after her, slightly shocked. She had acquired an employee.

That was something she certainly hadn't expected when she had planned this open day.

Alistair arrived bright and early for his appointment on the following Satur-day morning, and Bonnie wrapped him in a protective gown as soon as he stepped over the threshold.

She had to stifle a laugh at his look of horror. She didn't make a habit of making her customers uncomfortable but the contrast of this big farmer in a black nylon hairdresser's gown couldn't have been more striking.

'What's this?' The tone was unashamedly one of alarm, but he still bent his head towards her so she could tuck a towel around his neck. He didn't look too sure about the whole thing, but let her guide him to the sink.

'Sit,' she commanded, 'and I'll get started washing your hair.'

The suspicious glint in his eyes deepened.

'I normally get a dry cut at the barber's.'

'That's not how we do things here.'

She told him about Lianne as she lathered the shampoo and massaged it into his head.

His eyes were closed and he was so still she wasn't even sure if he'd fallen asleep.

As she watched him, his eyes slowly fluttered open, and he stared at her for a moment. Then his slow grin had her heart racing.

'That has to be the most relaxing wash my hair has ever had. You're good at that.'

She felt a slow smile engulf her face, pleased by the unexpected compliment.

'Years of practice,' she said, grinning back as she towelled his hair dry.

'You could do worse than employ Lianne,' he said while she began to comb out his hair. 'She's well liked around these parts, and I've heard she's a hard worker.'

'I had a feeling she'd be good for the salon,' Bonnie said, working hard to maintain a detached demeanour as she met his glance in the mirror. 'But it's good to have you confirm that.'

It was true. Somehow, and for some reason, she was keen to hear what he had to say. Which surprised her. Bonnie didn't make a habit of seeking the approval of anyone else — particularly not when it came to running her business.

But Alistair had given her sound advice up until now. And solid practical help.

She thought back to the time she had been stuck in the mud. If it hadn't been for him she would have completely missed the appointment she had set up with Daisy.

Word would have spread that she was unreliable. Her business would have failed before it had even properly started.

Instead, she now had the promise of a thriving living here. And she had Alistair to thank — for pulling her from the mud so she could keep her appointment with Daisy, for the idea of an open day, and for persuading customers through the door on the day.

'Sit still,' she commanded, as she picked up the scissors. 'Now, let's see if I can do something with that hair.'

The fact that his opinion mattered so much worried her. And, even more concerning, she knew she was beginning to trust him.

And he seemed to trust her.

With his hair, if nothing else.

No Chance of Romance

Alistair was in a surprisingly good mood when he arrived back at the farmhouse after his haircut. Bonnie had been kind to his hair, and had only tidied up his unruly curls, rather than shearing them off completely as his barber normally did.

But it wasn't only that. He had actually enjoyed his visit to the salon, something he didn't think he would ever have admitted to, not even to himself.

She had even made him a cup of tea, and provided chocolate biscuits. His barber never did that.

He suspected, though, that his good mood had more to do with spending time with Bonnie rather the actual treatment his hair had received, or the refreshments she had provided.

His barber never smiled at him the

way Bonnie did. Alistair grinned at the memory.

In his opinion, Bonnie had done such a good job that not even Ailsa would be able to find fault. And, given that she had warned him to be smart for this wedding later today, he knew she would be extremely fussy.

He sighed as he went to get ready. He still wasn't convinced that accompanying his sister's friend was wise. Or even that going to the wedding at all was a good idea.

When the invitation had arrived, Alistair hadn't given it much thought. It hadn't seemed right to go to an ex-girlfriend's wedding, even if their romantic relationship had been brief and the friendship preceding it had been long.

When pressed to respond, he had expressed regret to Daisy. He had, he told her, another engagement that day. Not that he had elaborated, but he and Jess would be out in the fields as they generally were on a Saturday afternoon.

Never had he expected to be getting dressed up in his best suit — his only suit if he was honest — and preparing to meet Ailsa's friend so he could act as her plus one.

It had meant a back-tracking phone call to his ex.

'Of course it's not a problem to change your mind, Alistair,' Daisy had assured him when he'd phoned her to check. 'I'll be pleased to see you there. I was disappointed when you turned down your invitation.'

Very civilised, Alistair had thought ruefully, his last hope of an excuse to refuse Ailsa's request evaporating.

That had been the favour his sister had required. The price for her bringing her friends to the open day at Bonnie's salon.

It had been worth it though, because the result had meant the open day had been a success. Bonnie had assured him when he went for his haircut this morning that, even if her appointments book wasn't exactly full to bursting just yet, she now had a healthy list of clients.

The thought of Bonnie made him smile again.

She would be at the wedding, she had said.

He would rather be going with her.

Alistair coughed — suddenly feeling as though he was choking.

He had tied his tie too tight and he hurriedly loosened it — and his collar. He was so out of practice at wearing formal wear that he had forgotten how to put it on — or how uncomfortable it was. A formal suit was as alien to him as a tutu would have been to a deep-sea diver.

This was the price he had to pay for securing Ailsa's help at Bonnie's open day. And it was worth it. What were a few hours of discomfort compared to a flying start for Hairdos of Shonasbrae? Even if weddings weren't his thing at all — especially not one as fancy as Daisy would probably be planning.

That was one of the reasons he had known straightaway that things wouldn't work out between the two of them. She was apt to like a fuss and relished drama, whereas he wanted a quiet life.

He wondered if that was another item he should add to his list.

Then he thought about Bonnie, about how she was likely to like a fuss, too, working as a beautician. Not that he knew much about the job, but he imagined there would be a lot of drama in a salon.

He suddenly decided that his ideal woman being fond of a quiet life was a requirement that he didn't need.

For the right woman, he would put up with a fuss.

And he was proving that today, because if it wasn't for Bonnie there would have been no danger of his agreeing to suffer the fuss of going to Daisy's wedding.

★　★　★

Bonnie rifled through her wardrobe and eventually decided on a pink shift dress, with contrasting darker pink jacket and matching dark pink shoes.

Shoes she had thought were the perfect finishing touch to the outfit when she'd bought them, but now, faced with the whole ensemble reflected in the mirror of her wardrobe, she frowned. Despite her well-styled shining hair, she reminded herself of a certain teenage doll. One who was often dressed in pink.

There was little choice, though, and she was lucky she had an outfit that was even remotely suitable at such short notice, her work skirt suits being too severe and work-like for a wedding. Her casual clothes were decidedly too casual for such an occasion.

She hadn't planned to go to the wedding, or else she would have bought something especially for it. The invitation had come as a surprise. When Bonnie had confirmed final arrangements yesterday for hair and make-up,

Daisy had pleaded with her to share the day.

'It would be great,' Daisy said, her eyes alight with obvious excitement. 'Everyone will be there. Even Alistair changed his mind in the end.'

At the mention of his name, Bonnie was rather alarmed to find her heart lurched — and she struggled to keep a disinterested expression. It wouldn't do for Daisy to get the wrong idea.

An invitation to the actual ceremony and reception wasn't normal, she was sure, for anyone who only knew the bride because she had been engaged to do the bridal make-up. Bonnie didn't think it was wholly professional to accept, but Daisy had put forward the very convincing argument that she would be happier to have her there in case her make-up smudged.

She was being kind, Bonnie was sure, inviting the new woman in town so she would be included in what was certain to be Shonasbrae's event of the decade. But even if the offer had been motivated by pity, Bonnie didn't want to throw that kindness back in her face.

'Well . . . ' she began uncertainly. 'If you're sure I wouldn't be in the way.'

'You'd positively be helping,' Daisy had insisted. 'I'd be a lot happier with my right-hand make-up woman by my side. There's a space at the table where Zac and Lianne will be sitting. You know them, don't you?'

Bonnie nodded, suddenly keen once she knew she'd be sitting with people she knew — particularly Lianne.

Even if she would have preferred to be seated next to Alistair, she knew it would have been rude to have said so.

As she surveyed her reflection now in the full-length mirror in her bedroom, she decided she didn't look at all bad, if you could get over all the pink.

She had bought this outfit to go to an awards ceremony — her old boss had been nominated for a most innovative business person award, and had asked Bonnie to go along to the dinner, for company.

Despite high expectations, Nita hadn't won.

The evening had taught Bonnie a valuable lesson — to take nothing for granted. But it seemed it had taught Nita very little. The other woman had still been subjecting everyone to her impossibly high and mighty ways when Bonnie had left.

Really, it was a wonder Nita had any customers left.

Bonnie sighed. She wished her old boss well, of course she did, she had learned everything she knew from the other woman after all. But she couldn't pretend she wasn't pleased to be away from the high drama of everyday life in Nita's salon.

Bonnie didn't believe in drama for the sake of it. All she wanted was to create a relaxing customer experience — build a business where people would want to come back. And she knew she could do it, too.

This week's small surge in customer numbers had proved that. All she had to do now was to keep the momentum going.

Being a part of local life would help towards that. So how could she turn down the chance that Daisy had kindly given her to integrate today? Even if it meant she would be effectively gate-crashing an occasion where she barely knew more than a handful of people. Oh well, at least she knew the bride and bridesmaids were lovely. And Alistair would be there.

That last thought made her smile.

And why shouldn't it? Despite knowing him such a short time, she liked him very much. As a friend, of course. Even if she had liked him as more than a friend, she had no time for romance and a man complicating her business plans.

Even if she did decide a flirtation might be nice, she wasn't about to settle in Shonasbrae for ever. She was keeping her eye on the bigger picture and the chain of salons that she planned across the country.

So how could she even consider allowing herself to fall for Alistair when he was so very much a dedicated farmer and settled in Shonasbrae?

He was unlikely to want to move with her when she moved on. Any romance between them would be doomed before it even started.

She pushed those uncomfortable thoughts from her mind and picked up her pink clutch bag along with her make-up case.

She had to put an end to this nonsense. There was no time for a flight of fancy when there was work to be done.

Daisy's Wedding

Alistair was outside in the farmyard, ready and waiting, when Ailsa and Gilly came to collect him.

'This is good of you, Alistair,' Gilly, an imposing redhead, cricked her neck to smile at him from the front seat as he folded his frame into the back of Ailsa's tiny car. 'I'm not normally a coward, but the thought of turning up to that wedding without a plus one makes me ill.'

Alistair resisted the urge to point out that he had an invitation in his own right, so he technically wasn't a plus one. He also resisted the urge to comment that Gilly didn't look as though she'd be frightened of anything. Or anyone. Ever.

But he couldn't help but feel a twinge of sympathy. Ailsa had told him the breakup was fresh and it was obvious from her reluctance to go to the wedding on her own that Gilly wasn't over it.

In the church, they sat a few rows from the back, Alistair uncomfortable in his suit, and wedged between his sister and her friend as they waited for the bride to arrive.

'Alistair, do sit still and stop fidgeting with that collar,' Ailsa hissed.

With a sigh, he reluctantly forced himself to stop trying to loosen his tie any further.

In the forefront of his mind was the fact that Bonnie would be arriving at any moment, if indeed she wasn't already here.

It was hard work attempting to keep his frequent visual sweeps of the guests as casual as possible. He didn't want Ailsa to notice and start asking awkward questions, but he couldn't help worrying he might have missed Bonnie.

He knew she had said she would be attending, but what if she'd changed her mind? She'd told him, when she cut his hair this morning, that she was worried that she hardly knew anyone who was going.

He had assured her he would be a friendly face in the crowd — someone to talk to, if things became unbearable. Though, in that respect, he maybe needed her more than she needed him.

Formal occasions weren't really to his taste. Neither was the formal suit that was still bothering him.

He made another effort to ignore how tight his collar was. He didn't want to get into his sister's bad books again.

He was much more comfortable in jeans — which was one of the very good reasons why he had taken the opportunity to take over the running of the farm instead of taking up the place he had been offered to study engineering at university.

It wasn't a decision he had ever regretted. He couldn't imagine a life spent indoors when he had the option of spending each day with the wind blowing through his hair.

A cool shiver tickled the back of his neck, now a little barer than it had been first thing this morning — before Bonnie had set to work.

He turned, just in time to see her slipping quietly into a pew behind him. She was late. That would be why he hadn't seen her up until now.

But then she had been working — probably fussing over Daisy until the very last moment.

Their eyes met briefly and he smiled.

He didn't think he'd ever seen so much pink in his life.

As she fussed with getting her dress to lie just right across her knees, he imagined she would smell like the exotic flower she reminded him of.

It seemed unfair in the extreme when he had promised to be here to keep Gilly company, but he wanted to squeeze out of his pew and go and join Bonnie.

Before he could act on that impulse — if he ever would have done — Ailsa nudged him sharply in the ribs.

'Alistair,' she hissed. 'Stop fidgeting.'

Before he could reply, there were suddenly flashing of cameras and the organ changing to play a new tune that signalled the arrival of the bride.

He had missed his chance. He was trapped here with Ailsa and Gilly for the duration of the ceremony.

★ ★ ★

The marquee that had been set up in Daisy's parents' garden was full to bursting with people enjoying themselves.

There was only one thing that marred the occasion as far as Bonnie was concerned — she hadn't been able to get anywhere near Alistair all day. As one of the few friendly faces she knew at the event, she had hoped to be able to at least chat with him for a while.

Maybe, if she was feeling bold, she might even have admitted that she had hoped for a dance with him.

When she had cut his hair earlier, he had seemed pleased that she was going. And that had pleased her.

If she was honest with herself, she had been looking forward to seeing him. And her heart had skipped a completely irrational beat when she had spotted him in his smart suit, sitting in the row ahead of hers in church.

He scrubbed up rather well.

Not that he didn't look good in his work clothes, too, because he did.

Despite her hopes of speaking to him, however, he was closely guarded by his sister's friend. They were either chatting, or dancing, or laughing together — effectively freezing Bonnie out at every turn.

Not that Alistair hadn't warned her about Gilly, but Bonnie had hoped for a chance to chat to him nevertheless.

He had confessed that Ailsa had talked him into accompanying her friend when Bonnie had cut his hair earlier. He hadn't seemed too happy about the arrangement.

It was a favour, he had said. He had promised it was to be a casual arrangement and that there would be plenty of time for him to socialise with his friends. And he had assured Bonnie that she would be top of the list of people he would be looking forward to chatting with.

She sighed.

It looked as though he'd changed his mind.

Not that she was watching them especially, of course. But he and Ailsa's friend were easy to spot as they moved around the dance floor together. They made a striking couple. Both were tall, her red hair contrasting with his now neat, dark curls.

Bonnie frowned. She should be happy that this blind date was working out. He was her friend — one of her few friends in Shonasbrae — and she wanted him to be happy. But she suddenly realised that she didn't want him to be happy with this Gilly. Not romantically, at least.

That didn't make sense.

Not unless she wanted him herself.

'Good wedding.' At her side, Zac attracted her attention and held up his glass to her.

'Yes, it is.' She smiled as the others around them all cheered and held up their glasses. She'd been put on the singles table — the fun table. Apart from Zac, she was pleased to see Lianne there, too.

Who needed Alistair when she had these outgoing and lovely people to chat to?

Certainly not Bonnie, she told herself fiercely, which was just as well as he was still engrossed in whatever chat the lovely Gilly was involving him in as they danced around the floor.

Not that Bonnie was looking at him, of course.

She wasn't taking the slightest notice of how they moved so naturally, how gently he held Gilly in his arms, how his head moved closer to hers as they laughed together . . . And she was completely oblivious to what a very handsome couple they made.

Bonnie sighed and made a huge effort to concentrate on the goings-on at her own table.

Whoever Alistair did or did not dance with was none of her business. But the conversation going on around her was.

Lianne was holding court, telling them all an amusing story about her son and his friends who had recently been on a survival weekend in the hills with their school.

'Mud everywhere when he came back,' Lianne told the listening crowd. 'I had to throw his walking boots and socks in the bin — they were beyond redemption.'

Bonnie could well believe it. Her own shoes had suffered the same fate after the incident with her car and the mud. She would never have thought it possible before she had moved to Shonasbrae.

She dutifully smiled as Lianne checked the reaction around the table.

Seeing now how her new employee integrated with the other guests, how everyone seemed to like her, how bright and cheery she was, even when reciting this tale of footwear woe, Bonnie was more sure than ever that the other woman would be an asset to the salon.

As the others took their turn to speak, and as the funny stories and jokes made their way around, Bonnie found she was truly enjoying herself. She laughed until her sides hurt.

And she hadn't checked on Alistair for a while. At least five minutes.

As she tried to regain her composure, Zac leaned towards her so he could be heard above the noise.

'Fancy a dance?'

Despite herself, she glanced again towards where Alistair and Gilly were dancing. It didn't seem as though he would be free any time soon, and she did like to dance . . .

'Thank you, Zac. I would.'

For such a tall lad, he was a

remarkably good dancer and Bonnie found she enjoyed herself far more than she had expected to in his company.

It only seemed like five minutes later that Daisy approached them.

'Sorry.' The bride grimaced apologetically at Bonnie and Zac. 'I hate to break up the party, but I wonder if you wouldn't mind freshening up my make-up? I feel I've been kissed by so many guests I won't have any left on.'

'You're still every inch the gorgeous bride,' Bonnie assured her with a smile, 'but maybe we could apply a touch more lipstick.'

* * *

Once they were in Daisy's room, it was pretty evident that the bride wanted a chat more than she wanted help with her make-up.

'I've been so worked up about today,' she said as Bonnie reapplied lipstick. 'I just want everything to be perfect.'

'It is perfect,' Bonnie reassured her.

'You look lovely, your groom is handsome, everything is just right.'

Daisy smiled.

'I think we'd have been better off eloping — just the two of us on a beach somewhere. Getting married in front of so many people I've known all my life is lovely, but there's nowhere to hide if things go wrong.'

'But nothing has gone wrong.' Bonnie stood back to admire the repairs to Daisy's make-up.

Bonnie was surprised to see the normally self-assured Daisy so worked up over an event where everyone held nothing but goodwill for her in their hearts. But that worked both ways, it seemed, and it was lovely to see that Daisy was so worried about her guests enjoying themselves.

'This is your day,' Bonnie reminded her as they prepared to leave Daisy's room and rejoin the party, 'and everyone is so happy for you both. All you have to do is enjoy yourself.'

Daisy smiled.

'You're right. I'm being silly. Thank you.'

'Not silly at all — it's normal to be nervous.'

Daisy gave her a quick hug.

'Thanks, Bonnie. I don't know what I'd have done without you today.'

Bonnie knew she hadn't done anything, but arguing the issue wasn't high on her list of priorities. She was pretty sure Daisy wouldn't listen, in any case.

'Come on. Let's get you back to your guests. They'll be wondering where you are.'

★   ★   ★

Zac had moved his attentions to one of the younger women by the time Bonnie arrived back at the table. She smiled as she noticed them on the dance floor. She had been grateful for his company, but she hadn't expected he would stay by her side all evening.

The others had all abandoned the table, too — a couple of them at the bar and the others making their way around the dance floor with various partners.

She was cross with herself when she looked out for Alistair, and was inexplicably upset when there was no sign of him — only because he was one of the few people she knew well enough to look out for, she insisted to herself, but still it would have been better if she hadn't cared at all.

In a minute she would go and fetch herself a drink, but for now she was content to sit and watch the celebrations.

'Seems like your boyfriend has found a new dancing partner,' a voice spoke in her ear and a shiver ran down her spine.

Alistair.

She didn't even need to turn her head to be sure. She would have recognised his voice anywhere.

His words suggested he knew she had been dancing with Zac, so he might have been watching her as closely as she had been watching him. That thought made her smile.

'And where has your girlfriend gone?' She attempted to keep the tone light, not wanting him to know how miffed she was that he had been paying such close attention to another woman all evening — even if that other woman was the reason he was here at all.

'She left me for another man.' He grinned. 'Thank goodness.'

She glanced up sharply and found his blue eyes full of amusement — and she followed his gaze to where Gilly was paying far too much attention to a tall, red-haired man.

'Her ex,' Alistair supplied. 'It seems I was being used to make another man jealous — and it worked.'

He sat down in the empty seat beside her and Bonnie stared at him, open-mouthed.

'That's terrible, Alistair.' She was appalled.

He laughed.

'I don't think it was quite that calculating. Gilly genuinely didn't want to come here on her own when she knew he was going to be here. And it seems that once he saw her again, he realised he'd made a mistake calling things off.'

Bonnie sighed.

'I hope things work out for them.'

'Me, too.'

She glanced at him again. His words seemed sincere.

'Do you really?'

His gaze met hers and she felt a little giddy.

'Of course I do. Why wouldn't I?'

'It was only . . . the two of you seemed a little cosy on the dance-floor — laughing and joking and getting along like a house on fire.'

'You seem to have been taking a lot of notice of what we were up to.'

'You were difficult to miss. As the tallest couple in the marquee, nobody could have avoided seeing you.'

He threw back his head and laughed.

'I suppose we were. But if you'd been taking as much notice as you say, you'd have noticed that she was the one doing the dancing and dragging me along with her.

'She was the one both telling the jokes and also the one laughing at them. And she was the one trying a little too hard to show what a good time she was having.'

'Sounds like she was out to catch someone's eye.'

'It would seem so.'

'And you're sure it wasn't you she was trying to impress?'

'Of course not.' He shook his head. 'Her ex-boyfriend couldn't keep his eyes off her and came to claim her as soon as he could.'

Bonnie smiled.

'That sounds quite romantic.'

'According to Ailsa, there was nothing romantic about it when they broke up. But she seemed determined to show him she wasn't affected by his being here — even though it was obviously not true.'

'A broken heart will do that to you.'

He shrugged a broad shoulder.

'I wouldn't know.'

She found that hard to believe. A man like Alistair was bound to have relationships in his past and, as he was single now, that would suggest the relationships hadn't lasted.

But if it was true that his heart had never been broken, maybe Alistair had been the one breaking hearts.

Bonnie thought about that for a moment. He didn't seem the type of man who would be cruel. But even if he was, it was none of her business.

He held out his hand.

'As both our previous dance partners are otherwise engaged, would you dance with me?'

She didn't even hesitate for an instant before she took his hand and they walked to the floor together.

Definitely Not a Date

Alistair was pleased he had asked Bonnie to dance and even more pleased that she had accepted. Even if she was a woman he had deemed unsuitable as a farmer's wife, she seemed right for him in so many ways.

As he held her close and they danced to the slow beat of the music, his list no longer mattered. All he cared about was the here and now. How good it was to have his arms around her, and to have her head rest on his shoulder.

Even if, in the long-term, he was wasting his time — and hers — the sweetness of the moment meant a waste of time had never seemed to be more enticing.

On paper, Gilly had been perfect for Alistair.

'How are you settling down at Sheldonmill?' he had asked, trying to make conversation as they entered the marquee.

'Town's too busy for me,' she had confided, looking around for their table. 'I'm a country girl at heart.'

It turned out she had grown up on a farm very similar to Alistair's. And she had helped out about the place — and enjoyed every moment. Just the sort of woman he had hoped to meet when he had drawn up his list.

There would be no prospect of someone like Gilly being unhappy with the relentless work, the isolation, the dedication, and single mindedness needed to run a successful farm.

Really, he should have been glad to meet her. The thought that Ailsa might introduce him to a suitable wife was what he had secretly hoped for when he told his sister about his list.

But he felt nothing of the interest that should have been there.

And he knew that even if there hadn't been an ex-fiancé lurking in the background, complicating matters, he still wouldn't have been interested.

It had been grossly unfair to his companion, but his attention had been firmly fixed on Bonnie.

He had been aware of exactly where she was sitting. He had known when she laughed with her companions. He'd had to use all his willpower not to get up and join her at her table. And, when Zac had taken her in his arms and led her to the dance floor . . . Well, Alistair had never wished more that he could trade places with another man.

In fact, he had been so preoccupied with his dismal attempts to stop watching Bonnie's every move that he completely missed what was going on under his nose. Until it — or him, to be more exact — nearly hit him in the face.

Gilly, whether or not she had meant to, was attracting the attention of a young man from across the way. Tall and broad, he had a look about him that made Alistair think he and Gilly would make a fine couple — apart from the expression on his face.

By the time Alistair noticed him, he was storming over to them with a face like thunder. And Alistair was powerless to do anything to stop him.

Gilly had gripped Alistair's arm, as though she was looking for support.

'It's Mark,' she said, the blood draining from her already pale, red-head's complexion as her gaze fixed on the angry young man storming towards them.

He didn't need to ask who Mark was. Gilly's reaction said it all. Mark was the ex who Gilly had been so keen not to run into without moral support.

Alistair braced himself for trouble. But Mark didn't have eyes for anyone but Gilly.

'Dance with me?' he asked in a tone that made Alistair realise that the heartache of separation had definitely not been one-sided.

Mark wasn't angry — he was broken-hearted.

As Gilly took her ex-fiancé's hand

and followed him on to the dance floor, Alistair knew that his purpose here was over. The way the two were gazing at each other, he wouldn't be seeing Gilly back at the table any time soon.

He smiled, pleased that the couple seemed happy. He hoped they would be able to work out their differences now.

Once Gilly had willingly stepped back into her ex's arms, Alistair began to enjoy the wedding much more than he had expected to. His evening seemed suddenly brighter — without the twin spectres of forced conversation and even more forced dancing.

And he was free to follow his heart — for tonight at least.

For one evening, he could allow his undeniable attraction to Bonnie to surface. Everyone flirted and danced at weddings, so where was the harm?

But while he had been self-conscious of every step of every dance with Gilly, dancing with Bonnie was a completely different prospect.

Being with her was as natural as breathing.

He didn't want it to end.

But all good things did end eventually, and all too soon they were being gathered around to wish the newlyweds well as they headed to their honeymoon hotel, ready to jet set off early the next morning.

'Do you want a drink? Or shall we go straight back to the dancing?' Alistair asked as the band struck up and noisy revellers resumed the party.

'A drink first, I think.'

Alistair didn't argue with that. Dancing, particularly in an over-heated marquee was thirsty work and they found a corner to sit and enjoy their cooling drinks.

'What's happening with the farm while you're here?' she asked. 'The animals, I mean. Don't you have to go and see to them?'

'Hugh volunteered.' Alistair had been planning to use the animals as an excuse to get back, but that had been when he had thought he would be stuck with his sister and her friend.

When he realised he wanted to hang around to speak to Bonnie, he had been keen to take his farmhand up on the offer.

'I think he was well out of his comfort zone once the dancing started.'

She nodded.

'He did look a bit awkward — even more so than he did the other day at the salon.'

Alistair smiled at the reminder. He hadn't been too comfortable in the salon himself that day, but it had been a different prospect when he had gone back for his haircut.

They were silent for a while, both deep in thought.

'I was sitting next to Zac for the meal,' Bonnie told him eventually.

'I noticed.' He tried to make the words sound casual — as though he hadn't been watching her every moment he could. Because that was just creepy. And strange. And Alistair never did things like that. He was never so taken with a woman that his attention would be on her rather than on his official companion.

'He's a nice lad.' She took a sip of her drink, not quite meeting his eye, almost as though she was reluctant to praise another man in front of him. But that was daft. It would be his imagination playing tricks on him. Zac was a nice young man and there was no reason why she shouldn't comment on that.

'He is. A hard worker, too.' Never normally at a loss for words, Alistair was suddenly not sure of what to say to Bonnie. It was almost as though he was shy — which was ridiculous as he was never shy. Or maybe he was so keen to impress her, he didn't want to say the wrong thing. But that was equally ridiculous.

Luckily she didn't seem to notice. She finished her drink then smiled up at him.

'So,' she said, 'another dance? Or,' she glanced towards the exit, 'maybe we could get some air? Take an evening stroll?'

He didn't hesitate. He put down his glass and followed her outside.

And he didn't even want to mention that her pink shoes were completely unsuitable for a country walk, in case she changed her mind.

A Night Just Right for Kisses

Dancing with Alistair had been more fun that it should have been — more than the sum of the parts, more than moving her feet in time to the music, more than the fleeting moments in his arms as they twirled and swayed to the beat, more than the shared laughter at nothing much.

Bonnie wasn't looking for romance in Shonasbrae, but with Alistair she felt as though she might have found it.

The cool evening air hit Bonnie right in the face as they stepped outside, and she was grateful to be able to breathe again. Too many dancing guests in the marquee made for a very hot and stuffy atmosphere in there.

The sky was darkening, but streaked with vivid reds and pinks.

'Shepherd says it will be nice tomorrow,' he joked, referencing the old saying.

She smiled. Every single day in Shonasbrae since she'd moved here had brought rain in some shape or form — which was why, of course, the place was so vividly green. Even today there had been a brief shower although, thankfully, it had dried up in time for Daisy's big day.

Bonnie took a deep breath, relishing the coolness of the evening.

She continued to tell herself that fresh air had been her only motivation for suggesting a walk. Of course it had been. There was no way she'd had an ulterior motive or hoped to get Alistair to herself.

Though, as they fell into step as they walked to the path that led away from the marquee, and his hand found hers, she knew in that instant that she was kidding herself.

The knowledge hit her like a sledgehammer. Despite Ailsa's warning that Alistair wouldn't be interested in someone like her, despite knowing that Alistair wasn't her type, despite the fact she knew she wasn't going to be in Shonasbrae long enough to form a meaningful relationship, she was sliding into very dangerous territory.

'Daisy's family have gone to a lot of effort for this wedding.' Bonnie glanced up at the trees that lined the pathway. Even though it wasn't quite dark yet, fairy lights twinkled down from them, giving the walkway a magical quality.

'Only the best for Daisy.' There was no bitterness in his voice and he smiled as he spoke.

'Of course, everyone wants the best for their children.'

They made their way to the river. The same river that wound its way around Alistair's land.

Daisy's parents had positioned a bench on the banks for quiet contemplation and that was where they made their way to now.

The laugher and music reached them across the evening air — albeit a bit more subdued that when they'd been in the marquee.

'Quite a party,' he said as they sat down.

She nodded.

'I'm glad I came. Daisy was right, everyone seems to be here.'

It seemed daft, to be making this sort of daft chitchat when there was so much more to say. He had let go of her hand now, and seemed as awkward as she was and she wondered if he knew, if only on some unconscious level, her sudden realisation.

'It's not normally like this, you know. Shonasbrae is a quiet town. We have simple tastes. That's why everyone's letting their hair down now they have the chance.'

'Everyone apart from Hugh,' she said quietly, mindful that the man had seemed to be out of his depth amongst the celebrating locals.

Alistair frowned at her words.

'He finds it difficult,' he said quietly. 'His wife died just a few years after they married. Zac was a baby. He's been wary of joining in ever since.'

'Poor man.' It was so very sad. Bonnie didn't quite know what to say.

'He spent his time working and raising their son. He always said he didn't have time for anything else. But Zac's an adult now, and he still keeps to himself, almost as though he's worried about being judged for being disloyal to her memory if he enjoys his life.'

'He must have loved her very much.'

'They were childhood sweethearts. Met at school and didn't spend a day apart since they married at nineteen.'

Bonnie wondered what it would be like to be loved like that. To die and to leave a man so heartbroken that life would stop for him, too.

She couldn't imagine it.

None of her relationships so far had developed into anything beyond friendship and that had been her choice. She wanted to be a successful businesswoman and she knew that would take most of her time and effort. What time would she have left to nurture a romance?

But now she had met Alistair, she began to see she might be able to live a different kind of life. Maybe she could have both a business and a husband and family of her own. Other women did, so why not her?

It was strange that it hadn't even occurred to her before.

She glanced across at Alistair, then looked down to where her hand rested in his on the bench between them and she gave a contented sigh. His fingers tightened around hers and she looked up to find his gaze on her mouth.

It was a night just right for kisses.

She leaned in closer — as did he.

Her heart skipped a beat and she forgot to breathe. Just at the moment when their lips might have met, a commotion occurred from somewhere behind them.

Alistair was the first to regain his

wits. He glanced back towards the marquee.

'It looks like the party's spilled outside.'

She bit back bitter disappointment.

'Probably just as well.'

'Yes.' His tone was as flat has hers. 'I've an early start in the morning in any case. The animals . . . I can't ask Hugh to take the early shift when he's already been working this evening.'

'Yes, of course.'

'So I'd best get off.' Despite his words, he seemed reluctant to leave.

She nodded, while not wanting to let him go. There had to be something she could say to make him stay a little longer but she couldn't think what. They had danced, they had chatted, they'd been out for a walk . . .

And they had so very nearly kissed.

He got to his feet. And still she could think of nothing to say. Just when she thought he was about to walk away, he turned.

'You're not working tomorrow?'

The salon wasn't scheduled to open, but she had planned to potter about, cleaning, doing admin — all the things that went on behind the scenes with a successful business.

She suspected admitting to these less than thrilling plans would kill this conversation stone dead. And that was the last thing she wanted to happen.

'The salon won't be open if that's what you're asking.'

His sudden smile nearly took her breath away. She smiled back — she couldn't help it.

'In that case,' he paused, as though not sure he should carry on, 'how would you like to spend the day on the farm?'

*   *   *

The shepherd had lied — or at the very least been mistaken. From the clearest sky at sunset that had spread the most vibrant pinks and reds across the sky and had promised a beautiful Sunday,

171

angry clouds had gathered overnight.

Alistair looked up at them now, the plans he had made for a happy day showing Bonnie his farm and holiday cabins disappearing before his very eyes as huge raindrops began to fall.

Normally he wouldn't have thought twice about a bit of rain. It was par for the course in Shonasbrae but he suspected Bonnie would be less than thrilled. He knew she would have fallen in love with the place if she had seen it on a sunny day. How could she not?

He frowned out of the window at the growing storm. But the rain poured on, unimpressed by his attempt to intimidate it.

As a farmer, a man accustomed to spending time outdoors, he had an inner instinct about the weather. But he hadn't seen this coming.

His heart sank at the same rate as the pelting rain. He had hoped to show his home to its best advantage, but he was going to have to drag her around a wet and muddy environment instead.

They would still have to plod on with his plans. The animals needed to be seen to, the chores still needed to be done.

Even though a large part of his income these days came from the properties he let on the land, there was no getting away from the fact that there were always pressing things to be done on a working farm.

Sunday didn't change that and neither did rain.

While he was keen to impress Bonnie, he also knew that a woman with no history in farming might well be horrified by the reality.

He wasn't even sure she would come. He wouldn't blame her if she didn't. To be honest, it might even be for the best if she didn't. He couldn't help thinking he'd been a bit rash inviting her to join him.

A girl like Bonnie, someone accustomed to the glamour and bright lights of city life, was hardly going to be impressed by a small farm with a handful of animals and a couple of cabins. The dirt, the smells — all so far removed from her fragrant life.

Just because he was proud of what he had built didn't mean anyone else would be impressed.

The sound of a vehicle pulling up outside made him realise how he'd been kidding himself when he had thought Bonnie cancelling their plans would be for the best. His heart leaped at the thought of seeing her.

He pulled on his boots, laughing as an excited Jess got in his way, then he went outside to find Ailsa getting out of her car.

'Didn't expect a reception,' she told him with a smile, bending to pat Jess's head.

'If I'd known it was you I wouldn't have bothered.' It sounded rude, but he didn't mean it that way. She'd grown up here and they didn't stand on ceremony for each other.

Disappointed she wasn't Bonnie, he turned and she and Jess both followed him into the house.

'Don't tell me,' Ailsa said, taking off her coat and shaking off the rain, 'expecting your little hairdresser, were you?'

He sighed.

'Don't be like that. She's nice.'

Ailsa's smile slipped.

'So you are expecting her?'

Alistair nodded.

'And what happened to your list?'

'I'm keeping it safe.'

'So you haven't changed your mind about it?'

He shrugged.

'Why would I do that?'

'Bonnie's not farmer's wife material. And wasn't it you who insisted you weren't going to bother dating in future unless the woman concerned was suitable?'

He couldn't believe how miserable it made him to admit it, if only to himself, but his sister was right.

'I'm not dating her.'

'And is she aware of that?' Ailsa was

looking at him carefully — no doubt trying as she often did to see how his mind worked. As his twin, she was often uncannily right. 'You'll get hurt, Alistair,' Ailsa told him gently, 'and, more to the point, so will she.'

He knew she was only speaking out of concern, but that didn't make him feel any better. And it definitely didn't make him feel better to know Ailsa was only reminding him to abide by his own rules. While he was big enough and ugly enough to look after himself, the last thing he wanted to do was to lead Bonnie on.

'I'm going to show her the farm,' he said, disappointment making his voice gruff, 'in the rain. And we're going to be working. It's hardly conducive to romance.'

'No,' she said, 'I suppose not.' She was thoughtful for a moment. 'And what about Gilly?'

'What about her?'

'Are we really going to have this conversation now?'

'Gilly should have been perfect for you.'

It seemed they were.

'Possibly she might have been. If she wasn't in love with her ex.' He hardly thought he needed to put that little snippet on his list. A woman not in love with another man would be a requirement for most people, he should imagine. 'Besides, you asked me to go as her plus one yesterday, so she wouldn't have to face him alone — not because you saw her as an ideal partner for me.'

Ailsa flushed slightly.

'You're so busted.' He shook his head, a reluctant smile appearing at his sister's cheek. 'You were matchmaking. And you suggested I take Gilly to that wedding before you even knew about my list. You need to stop meddling in other people's lives, Ailsa.'

'Just be careful with Bonnie.' Ailsa refused to take the advice. 'I know you. I know you'll be getting ideas and then when she can't live up to them it will be the end of the world.

'I really don't agree with your stupid list, but to be honest it's not a bad idea to keep to criteria you know you would be compatible with. You want to give any relationship a chance to last. As you said the other day, neither of us is getting any younger.'

With that, she turned and picked her coat off the back of the chair where she'd put it.

'Where are you going?'

'Back home before your lady love arrives. I don't want to play gooseberry to whatever might or might not be going on between the two of you.'

And with that she went back out into the rain.

A Farm Visit

'Yes, Nita,' Bonnie spoke into her phone with one eye on the time. 'It's terrible. But I'm sure you'll soon have him trained up.'

She needed to go. She should have been at Alistair's place by now.

Nita wasn't happy. When Bonnie had left to start up on her own, her boss had predicted tears.

However, far from being the one sitting back waiting for Bonnie to fall flat on her face, it was Nita who had reached out to renew their acquaintance.

'Darling, won't you leave that uncivilised place and come back to us?' Nita pleaded, having already exhausted the list of how Bonnie's replacement was falling short of expectations.

Keen to end this call, Bonnie sighed down the line.

'Nita, I've spent a lot of money on this place. I'm only just starting to become established. I really can't just give up. Not so soon, in any case.'

'It's you I'm thinking of. Your career will die a death out there. Those country people won't appreciate how talented you are, or how lucky they are to have you.'

Bonnie bit back a smile. When she had worked for Nita, the older woman had been guilty of those very crimes.

In fact, it wasn't just Bonnie she took for granted — her entire staff had complained of being undervalued. And it seemed, from her reports of how Bonnie's replacement was lacking, Nita hadn't changed her ways.

Nita was, however, one of the best in the business, so she was forgiven a certain arrogance and, to be truthful, her staff thought the world of her.

It was a mark of how much Bonnie wanted to go to see Alistair that she was keen to cut the conversation short.

'Nita, look, I'm sorry — I have to go.

I'll phone you tomorrow for a proper chat.' She knew she owed the other woman a good deal — Nita had taught her everything she knew about the business — but she was already running late.

'Darling,' Nita whinged down the line. 'Think what I'm offering you — a glorious future . . . '

Luckily, Bonnie knew all about Nita's idea of a glorious future, and she wasn't even tempted — not when she had her own vision to fulfil — and especially not when going back to Nita's salon would mean leaving Alistair behind.

She took a sharp intake of breath.

How did he do that? Intrude on her thoughts uninvited?

'What do you say, Bonnie? The customers have been asking for you. They'll be so pleased to see you back.'

'Nita, I really can't discuss this now.' She had already given her old boss more time than she could afford, and she knew Alistair would be waiting and wondering where she was.

She had promised him she would be there and she didn't want to let him down.

'I'll give you a pay rise.'

'This isn't about money.'

'I'll double your previous salary.'

Bonnie took another deep breath. She hated to be rude to anyone, and particularly to Nita. The other woman might have been a demanding boss, with a questionable sense of self-importance, but Bonnie couldn't help liking her and was grateful to Nita for all the invaluable training she had given her. But in this case, it seemed that being assertive was her only option.

'I'm really sorry, I have somewhere I really need to be and I'm already horribly late. I'll ring you tomorrow,' she insisted, gently putting the phone down while Nita was still pleading her case.

Bonnie felt terrible. She had been unforgivably rude. But why did everything have to be such a drama with Nita?

She glanced at the clock and realised she didn't have time to worry about that now. She would call Nita tomorrow, just as she had promised. And she would apologise for not having had time to talk today.

As for the rest of today, she was going to concentrate on having a nice time at the farm. Even if it was raining. She grimaced as she made a mad dash to the car.

Rain seemed to be a regular feature of her life here. She hadn't thought there would be so much more than there had been in town. Or maybe there was a similar amount, but she hadn't noticed in town because there were so many things to do indoors.

Here, the outdoors played such an important part of life — probably because there was so little in the way of entertainment.

But still she'd turned down the chance to return to her old life when Nita had offered it. Maybe she was turning into a country girl after all.

Jess was restless and Alistair knew she wanted to go out.

'In a minute, girl,' he told her, offering her a pat. 'We just have to wait for Bonnie. She'll be here soon.'

At least he hoped she would be.

The thought occurred to Alistair that he should maybe be thinking of organising a search party.

He glanced at the clock. Bonnie was only half an hour late, but what if something had happened to her? The roads were wet and muddy, and she had already managed to get herself into bother once before while driving on them.

She hadn't phoned to cancel — and surely she would have called if she had decided not to come.

With a growing sense of unease, he realised that there was a real danger she might be in trouble again.

He would try phoning her mobile first, he decided, to see if she was OK.

If there was no reply, he would try the salon phone. Then, if he still couldn't get hold of her, he would head out to see if he could find her. If she had got into difficulty, there was every chance she was in an area with no mobile signal.

His own landline sprang to life before he could put even the first part of that plan into action. The number had been withheld, but some sixth sense warned him it would be Bonnie.

The knock at the door as he squinted at the phone's display did surprise him, though.

He pressed the button to answer the call as he went to answer the door, trying not to be distracted by Jess getting entangled in his feet.

'Alistair speaking,' he said, feeling almost giddy with relief as he realised she had to be OK if she was managing to use the phone.

He was greeted with a sound of static and he frowned.

'Hello? Bonnie? I can't hear you . . . '

Jess yelped and barked enthusiastically as she followed him along the hall, his phone pressed tightly to his ear.

Whoever it was must be pretty brave to knock again with all the noise the dog was making.

He was still trying to make out Bonnie's voice on the line as he threw the door open.

His shock at finding Bonnie on the doorstep when he had expected to be speaking to her on the phone rendered him momentarily speechless.

'Aren't you going to ask me in?' she asked, rainwater running off the hood of her waterproof jacket on to her face.

She looked adorable. He wanted to scoop her up and kiss the raindrops from her nose. That shocked him even more than seeing her on his doorstep.

'You made it,' he said, knowing he sounded daft. 'I was beginning to think you'd decided not to come after all.'

'And why would I decide that?' she asked with a smile.

186

'The rain . . . Some people don't like it.'

'It would take a bit more than a few drops of water to put me off a plan.'

He resisted the urge to point out the obvious — that the storm they were encountering was definitely more than a few drops . . .

Still inordinately pleased she hadn't cancelled, he barely took any notice of the call. Until something finally broke through.

'Alistair, Alistair . . . It's Dan from next door. Can you hear me?'

'Dan, yes — good to hear from you. How are things?'

'Not too good. My Ettie's not well so I'm on my way to see her.'

'Sorry to hear that.' Alistair frowned. Ettie, Dan's sister, had always been good to Alistair and Ailsa and he was sorry to hear she was unwell.

'Listen,' Dan continued, 'I've stopped on the way to phone you. It's your sheep. They're out of the top field.

They're all over the road.' His neighbour's tone was urgent.

'My sheep?' Alistair asked incredulously.

'The fence is down. You'll need to repair it quickly. I'd stop to help, but . . . '

'Please don't worry, Dan. I know you'd help if you could. I appreciate that you let me know.'

Alistair was furious with himself. Finishing that last bit of fencing had been next on his list of jobs.

If only he'd got around to it last week, instead of leaving it for this, he would be able to enjoy his planned day with Bonnie, rather than having to put on his large waterproof coat and head up to the top field to see to the livestock.

'I'll come with you,' Bonnie said when he suggested she might wait for him at the farmhouse.

'You'll be more comfortable here, where it's warm and dry.'

She made eye contact, her gaze

trained on his face.

'I'm sure I'll be fine with you going up to the top field.'

She took his breath away.

He took a moment to collect himself.

'You'd be more comfortable here.' Her eyes were electrifying. Dark and mysterious. He couldn't look away. 'Rounding the sheep up and mending the fence is going to be pretty tedious to watch.'

'I'm sure it will be fascinating,' she told him taking a step towards him. 'I didn't come here to sit on my own in the house.'

The words just wouldn't form on his tongue. He wanted to ask her . . . to clarify exactly why exactly she was here.

'I came to spend the day with you.' It was almost as though she had read his mind. 'Seeing what happens on a working farm. And maverick sheep on the run sound pretty exciting to me.'

It seemed she wasn't about to be put off. Maybe she wasn't quite as high maintenance as he had suspected after all.

He smiled, the thought of his crumpled list making him smile at the suggestion Bonnie might tick one of the boxes on it.

And she was certainly dressed for a rainy day outdoors today. Her rain jacket would keep her dry — as would the very colourful wellies she was wearing.

'I got them to go to a festival a few years back,' she explained, blushing slightly as she noticed him looking at the pink and yellow boots on her feet.

'Festival?'

'A music festival,' she explained. 'They like to hold them in very muddy fields.'

Alistair grinned.

He couldn't imagine anything worse happening in his own muddy field, but he was more than impressed by the landowners who had diversified in that direction.

He nodded his approval.

'OK, then. Let's go before my sheep end up browsing the shops in Shonasbrae high street.'

Secret Plans Revealed

Once out in the yard, Alistair whistled an instruction to Jess, who raced to follow closely at his heels.

'I'll need her to round up the wandering sheep,' he explained, even though Bonnie hadn't asked, 'then I'll need to do what I can to secure the fence.'

He headed for the Land Rover. She was surprised they wouldn't be travelling in the tractor, but she was sure it would cover the muddy terrain admirably. It would also be more comfortable.

She shuddered as she remembered her brief trip in the tractor.

She wasn't quite sure what it was she had agreed to, but she knew it meant spending time with Alistair, so that was OK in her book.

'Do the sheep escape often?' she asked as they set off.

He glanced in her direction and grinned.

'Any chance they get. They like to wander — but then I suppose that's true of any animal if they're given the chance, isn't it?'

'I'm afraid I wouldn't know. I haven't had much to do with animals.'

She saw him grimace briefly and she wondered if she'd said something wrong. She briefly considered asking him, but before she got the chance a large building caught her eye as they drove past.

'What's that place?'

He glanced across.

'That's the barn. I've big plans for that.'

'Oh?'

That was all the encouragement he needed. As he negotiated the steep road up to the top field, he began to share his ideas for turning the barn into a wedding venue.

His enthusiasm was enthralling, and Bonnie was swept along — imagining brides and grooms arriving at the beautiful old barn that was situated on the banks of the currently raging river.

'The photos will be lovely,' she said, thinking out loud. 'If it stops raining long enough for the bridal party to get outside.'

Alistair grinned.

'Believe it or not, we do occasionally see the sun. But you know that — we saw it briefly yesterday.'

She smiled at the reminder of the day that had ended so beautifully.

'What made you think of a wedding venue?'

He shrugged a broad shoulder, his blue eyes seeming to hold a guarded look as he glanced quickly over to Bonnie before turning his attention back to the road.

'It will complement the lodges,' he told her. 'I'm thinking of offering packages — the whole deal, including accommodation for the bridal party, so that the bride and groom can be saved from the stress.'

'Isn't that part of the fun of getting married?'

He seemed startled.

'Well, they would still have some input if they wanted, of course, but I'm hoping to go into partnership with photographers, clothing outlets, people who would come here to save busy couples having to chase around after everyone.'

'Fair enough. I'm sure there are people who would love that kind of service.' She smiled. 'Might you be looking to include make-up and hair for the bridal parties?'

'Maybe I will.'

'Then maybe I'll pitch to be included.'

'I'd like that,' Alistair said, suddenly serious. 'I think we would work well together.'

Bonnie had only meant it as light-hearted banter, but she realised that she would like to work with Alistair, too.

'How far along are your plans?'

'Early stages. Some neighbours got

together to help me clear the barn a wee while back. And I've been buying up the odd thing that might be useful.'

She smiled.

'I like how things are around here,' she said. 'Everyone helping each other out.'

'Unlike the city.' He glanced sideways at her.

'Everyone's so busy there — too wrapped up in their own lives to notice neighbours.' Not that people wouldn't help in a crisis, but you were much more likely to rely on friends and family, rather than neighbours whose proximity was more down to accident than design.

'There they are.' Alistair pulled into the side of the road and turned off the engine.

Bonnie was aware of the rain beating on to the windscreen with renewed vigour and now that the wipers had stopped, it was difficult to see anything.

She jumped out, pulled her hood up

over her hair, and went to stand beside Alistair.

The sheep were dotted around the road, each doing their own thing like little woolly mavericks. Bonnie was surprised at how lively they were.

'I though sheep just stood there,' she said as she watched, 'in the field, eating grass.'

Alistair just laughed.

'I wish that were true. It would've saved us coming all the way up here today.'

He called instructions to Jess, and Bonnie watched in complete fascination as each and every sheep was rounded up and returned to the field.

'Goodness, that was amazing.'

He nodded in agreement.

'She earns her keep.'

This was turning out to be a revelation. Of course, she'd known in theory how a dog could round up sheep, but seeing it in practice at such close quarters was quite another thing.

Once the livestock were safe, it didn't

take him long to secure the fence. Bonnie liked to think she helped, but really she just stood there — exactly as she'd accused sheep of doing. But Alistair didn't seem to mind her being there and she was pleased about that. At least she wasn't in the way.

But they were both drenched as they made their way back to his Land Rover.

He drove her past the little cluster of holiday cabins on the way back.

'Six of them,' he declared proudly, 'but I hope there will be more soon.'

Her head was reeling with his plans. She'd thought herself a proactive business person, but compared with Alistair her planning was positively sedate.

'And are the cabins occupied just now? I haven't been aware of any guests since I saw that family leaving.'

He shook his head.

'There's nobody staying at the moment. I kept this week free of paying guests. I need to freshen the cabins up — a deep clean, a lick of paint . . . I'm expecting visitors — fussy visitors who will be looking for anything out of place.'

She hadn't been expecting that. She glanced at him, guessing there was more.

'Visitors?' she prompted. She wondered what made these visitors more remarkable than the others who had stayed at the farm since she'd met him. And why it was so important to impress them?

He nodded.

'They make an annual visit. I don't have a date yet for when they'll be here, but it's always around about this time of year. They want me to sell up. I have to convince them that it's a good idea to keep the place going.'

'Who are these visitors?' she managed at last. 'Who wants you to sell your farm?'

She was outraged at this suggestion of an aggressive takeover — of a possible business coup by ruthless individuals within the holiday industry, who saw what he'd achieved here and wanted to crush his aspirations under the juggernaut of their own plans.

'My parents.'

'What?' Her head snapped around to look at him to see if he was joking.

He didn't seem to be.

'Oh.' That came like a shock out of the blue. 'I thought . . . ' She stopped — not quite knowing how to carry on. How could she tell him she'd assumed his parents were dead? Not the kind of thing you should really say to anyone. But he had never mentioned them before, not in the present tense at least.

'Where do they live? Near here?' She thought that unlikely — she would have expected to have heard of them if they were local.

'They live abroad,' he said. 'In France. They took off when I was eighteen.'

'They just left you here? You and Ailsa? When you were both so young?'

'Mum hated the farm,' Alistair

confided. 'She hated the long hours and the low pay. She hated the mud and the outdoors. In the end, I think she resented it more than she liked being a wife and mother.'

Bonnie was appalled, though she tried not to let it show.

'Dad promised her that if she could wait until we grew up, then they could reconsider their lifestyle.'

'So they up and left?'

He had her full attention now and she was surprised when he turned off the engine. She hadn't even realised that they'd stopped.

Confused, she looked out to see the barn they had passed earlier, and the fast-flowing river. She wanted to ask why he had brought her here, but Alistair seemed to want to tell her more of his family's history.

'They wanted us to go, too. But Ailsa had her place to train as a nurse. I'd been offered a place on an engineering course, but I decided I'd rather stay on the farm. So I convinced them to keep the farm on, that it would be in their best interests.

'I used some money I'd inherited from my grandparents and a loan from the bank to buy a half share, so they had funds to travel with. But I'm always very conscious that they're keen to sell up.'

'Which is why you've started the holiday business?'

'All farmers have to diversify these days to survive. But I've ploughed all my money into doing that, so I'm not ready to buy them out quite yet.'

'And the bank wouldn't help?'

'I haven't approached them,' he said.

'And I'd rather not, unless I really have to. The business gives my parents a good return on their half share and it will continue to do so if my plans work out. I'd prefer to keep our arrangement going so I know they have an income — money to live off.'

Alistair seemed to have a lot of responsibilities to others — to his employees, to his parents. It was little wonder he was so keen to see his farm thrive.

'Where does Ailsa fit into all this?'

'She wasn't interested in the farm. She couldn't wait to leave, in fact. Much like our mother.'

There wasn't a hint of bitterness about his words — he was merely telling Bonnie how things were, but she couldn't help but feel for him, trying to keep the family's home together while all around him were trying to escape.

'That's why,' he told her quietly, so quietly she had to lean towards him to make out his words as the rain pelted against the windscreen, 'I've decided that when I marry, the woman I choose for my wife will have to be a country girl at heart.'

Bonnie broke eye contact, glancing involuntarily down at her decidedly un-country-girl footwear.

She couldn't help but feel he was issuing some sort of warning. One that she had no choice but to heed.

Even though the thought of marrying

Alistair had never occurred to her, she couldn't help but feel slightly miffed that she didn't have a choice in the matter.

That even if she had wanted him for a husband, he would never want her for his wife.

★ ★ ★

There. He'd said it. Put it out there. Left no room for error or misinterpretation.

Whatever he felt for her, whatever she felt for him, there was no denying the fact that they weren't right for each other.

Now he'd said the words out loud.

The look on her face, the crushed hope he hadn't even realised she'd harboured, tore at his heart and made him want to claw the words back.

But telling her had been the right thing to do. It was what he had decided. The fact that he needed to marry a country girl was number one item on his wife list. It was what he needed to do to protect his farm.

So why then did he feel so terrible about it?

'That river looks like it's about to burst its banks,' she said, her clumsy attempt at changing the subject revealing a lot more than it hid.

She was refusing to meet his gaze. Instead, her attention was turned away from him, and she was looking through the window and out at the view.

He didn't want her to be upset, of course he didn't, but the fact that she seemed so cool now, after her initial obvious disappointment, made him suspect his feelings for her were stronger than hers for him.

And maybe that was just as well. If it had been the other way around he couldn't have lived with the fact that he had hurt her.

He tore his gaze away from her and looked out towards the river that normally meandered sedately through his land.

Today it was on a furious rampage.

Only to be expected. The rain was relentless and had been for days now. The rise in the level of the river wasn't a surprise.

'It's high,' he agreed, 'but it hasn't overflowed in eighty years, so I think we're safe.'

She didn't look convinced.

'I've got a programme of work outlined to set in flood defences,' he added, 'just in case. It doesn't do to take nature's goodwill for granted and I wouldn't want this barn being flooded. Especially not when I'm storing stuff in there.'

That got her attention. Her head snapped around.

'What's in there?'

'Do you fancy a quick look?' He wanted to get away from the suddenly claustrophobic atmosphere in the Land Rover, while all the time aware that he had done this. He had broken the easy relationship that had been growing between them.

Her smile seemed decidedly forced. That made him sad.

'Yes,' she agreed. 'Let's make a dash for it. I think this rain's getting heavier.'

He knew a bit of rain didn't frighten her. She'd proved that in the top field as she'd helped him secure the fence.

Maybe, at heart if not by birth, she was a country girl.

Maybe. Would that be enough?

Alistair told himself to close that line of thought down right now. He didn't need to harbour false hopes where Bonnie was concerned.

The futility of his hopes for them had been the very reason for his declaration only moments ago — to put an end to all this nonsense so he could get on with his life. And to let Bonnie get on with hers.

But he couldn't help how he felt about her. He couldn't help the flicker of hope in his heart that, despite their very different ambitions and outlooks, there might be some way for them to make it work.

As they rounded the corner to the barn door, she gasped.

A pile of rubbish had been left outside the barn. Some of it he knew he would be able to sell for scrap metal — old machinery, equipment, bits of a tractor, and some unidentifiable paraphernalia that had been hanging the farm around since his grandparents' day.

'Oh my goodness.' Bonnie's shocked voice was barely more than a whisper, carried on the rain. 'That's a lot of . . . stuff.'

'Three generations — and more — of junk.' Alistair felt obliged to point out that this wasn't all his accumulated rubbish. 'And the last corner of the farm to be decluttered.'

It had been back-breaking work, but he had been determined to clear it. He needed the barn for storage.

'So what's in there now?' Bonnie asked again.

Alistair hesitated as the rain poured down on them both. He hadn't revealed his plans for the barn to anyone else — and showing her what was in there now was a step beyond talking but he wanted Bonnie to understand just how much of himself he was putting into the diversification of the farm.

Even as he worked that out, he knew she meant more to him than he cared to admit.

'Come and see.'

He held out his hand and she took it.

For someone that was so incompatible with his plans, her hand felt right in his.

He led the way and she gasped as he opened the door and his secret was revealed.

Tables, chairs, boxes of crockery and silverware and crystal glasses were stacked in the middle of the space.

He glanced across and saw an expression of surprise crossing her face.

'I saw this lot on an auction site. The price was too good to ignore. So I bought them.'

Bonnie looked around and he held

his breath as he waited for her verdict.

He knew there was a lot of work still to do, but the space was large and airy. It was important to him that she could understand his vision from these very basic beginnings.

'This looks like a bit more than early planning to me. It all looks wonderful.'

She smiled then, and in a blinding flash of clarity, the mental image struck him of Bonnie as a bride. Bonnie walking up the aisle here in this very barn, all the way to her waiting groom.

He knew then that he wanted to be that groom.

Some serious back-pedalling was needed from him if he was to recover from all the damage he had caused today and woo her.

Bonnie's Visitor

Bonnie was glad she had gone to the farm yesterday, even if she had arrived late and even if it hadn't quite turned out as the romantic day out she had imagined it would be when Alistair had invited her.

She had envisaged sunlit walks and maybe a picnic in a meadow as they sat by the gently rolling river.

Instead, she had been treated to an unvarnished glimpse of what her life would be like on Alistair's farm. Not that she was likely to need to know that — not when Alistair had made it clear she was not the type of woman he would be interested in making a lifelong commitment to.

With a sigh, she opened the blinds and gasped in surprise.

It wasn't raining.

There were still angry clouds, it was

true, but weak sunshine was trying to break through.

She got ready for work quickly and headed down to the salon. What with the results of the open day, plus Lianne's promise to talk to her friends, not to mention the networking Bonnie had herself done at the wedding, she was hopeful of a turn in her fortunes.

She had only been open for 10 minutes when the bell sounded to warn her the door had been opened and she ran through from where she'd been checking an order of shampoo in the back room.

'Ailsa,' she said, surprised to see Alistair's sister. 'I thought you'd be at the hospital.'

'Rare day off,' she said with a smile, 'though I think I could have chosen a better day for it — it's just started to rain again.

Bonnie glanced towards the window. The half-promise of sunshine that had made itself known earlier had completely vanished and there were spots of rain on the window.

With a sigh, Bonnie turned and smiled at her visitor — pen poised over the appointments book.

'What can I do for you today?'

'Nothing. I thought I'd pop by to see how you're settling in.'

Bonnie kept her smiled firmly pinned to her face, hoping it wasn't apparent how low her heart had sunk with those words.

Ailsa had been less than friendly the last time she had been in the salon. It was only natural for Bonnie to wonder if Ailsa was going to issue another warning about getting involved with Alistair.

'In that case, do you have time for a coffee?' she asked, good manners stopping her from demanding to know what Ailsa really wanted.

'I'd love one, thanks.' The smile was wide and seemed genuine. Bonnie decided to take it at face value.

'I wanted to apologise,' Ailsa came to the point without being encouraged to do so. 'I spoke out of turn at your open day. It's none of my concern who Alistair goes out with. I should have minded my own business.'

That took the wind right out Bonnie's sails.

'You were right to speak out,' Bonnie said. With the benefit of Alistair's statement yesterday, coupled with this apology, she knew now that Ailsa's warning had come from a good place — a place where not only had Ailsa been worried about her brother, but also concerned about Bonnie.

How could Bonnie be cross about something like that?

Ailsa shook her head.

'It's good of you to say, but I saw how Alistair was at Daisy's wedding. He seemed happy with you — happier than I've ever seen him before. If I've put a spanner in the romance works, then I'll never forgive myself.'

'There is no romance,' Bonnie admitted. 'We're friends. Nothing more. Like I told you last time.'

Ailsa shook her head.

'Not only did I see how Alistair looked at you,' she said, 'but I saw how you looked at him. If that wasn't romance then I don't know what is.'

'I was up at the farm yesterday,' Bonnie said, trying again not to wince as she saw the look of interest on Ailsa's face. 'Alistair had invited me. I wasn't quite sure what I was expecting, but I certainly wasn't thinking he would put me in my place by telling me outright that I wasn't countrified enough for his tastes.'

'Alistair told you that?'

'Not those exact words, but that was the gist of it.'

Ailsa shook her head.

'Sometimes,' she said, 'my brother doesn't know himself what's best for him.'

'And you think I'm what's best for him?' Bonnie was incredulous.

For a long moment, Ailsa looked at her, studying her carefully.

'It's taken me until now to realise it,'

she admitted. 'But yes. Yes, I do. Don't give up on him, Bonnie. He'll realise soon enough that you belong together.'

'And you've reached that conclusion how?'

The fact wasn't lost on Bonnie that it was only two days since Ailsa had set her brother up with her own friend. She had a history of meddling and it seemed she didn't give up.

'Based entirely on gut instinct.'

Bonnie stared at her.

'My gut instinct is rarely wrong,' Ailsa added.

'Gilly?' Bonnie reminded her gently.

'It would have been handy if they'd fallen for each other, but Gilly was never in the running for Alistair's heart. He was doing her a favour, so she wouldn't have to face her ex alone.'

'And you think I'm in the running for his heart?'

Ailsa nodded enthusiastically.

'I do.'

Despite wanting to believe it might be true, Bonnie couldn't help but think that this was taking a turn for the ridiculous. Who had this sort of conversation with someone they barely knew?

For a moment she was sure she had stepped into an alternate reality. Or maybe they just did things differently in Shonasbrae.

'And have you told Alistair this? Does he know you're here?'

'Good heavens, no.' Ailsa's eyes opened wide. 'I don't think he'd be amused somehow.'

'So you expect me to hang around and make a fool of myself, even though he's as good as told me he's not interested?'

'But he is interested. He's got it into his head that he needs a wife, and he's only willing to date women who have every requirement on that stupid list he's drawn up. He'll . . . '

It wasn't often Bonnie was lost for words, but she really didn't know what to say to this woman. This stranger who had happened into her salon not once, but twice in the space of a week, to try to run Bonnie's love life for her.

She wouldn't normally tolerate that sort of interference from anyone.

But she was interested in what Ailsa had to say about Alistair. How could she not be? Even if he had made it clear that any interest she had in him would be futile.

And Alistair had a list of what he was looking for in a wife? Bonnie really didn't know what to say to that.

'A list . . . ? He has a list of what he wants in a wife?' Without asking, Bonnie knew that she would have none of the attributes on this mythical list.

'Oh, gosh. I'm sorry.' Ailsa, to her credit, did look horrified. 'Forget I said that. Forget I said anything. It's just a daft thing. It doesn't mean anything.'

Only Bonnie knew it did.

Alistair had hinted as much yesterday and, even if Bonnie hadn't really been fussed one way or the other about finding a husband when she first moved to Shonasbrae, knowing she didn't meet the requirements on Alistair's list hurt.

And knowing about the list hurt even more. The fact Alistair had put his hopes in writing.

She stood stock still for a minute, too numb to react, knowing she would have to force herself to speak soon.

In the end she did what any self-respecting woman would do when faced with such a situation and she refused to be drawn into the matter.

'Can I fetch you a biscuit to go with that coffee?' She offered her most professional smile as she put a brave face on things.

But really she felt quite ill.

And it was only at that moment that she realised how much Alistair had come to mean to her. And now she knew for certain that there was no future for them, she wanted to weep.

No Time to Waste

Avoidance.

That was going to be Bonnie's word of the day for now.

She would avoid his calls.

Avoid his company.

Avoid him.

It was the only way.

And it worked to a certain extent. She managed to avoid him for the next two days — until he arrived in her salon, all casual jeans and broad shoulders in his black T-shirt, and her good intentions were washed down the sink along with the warm soapy water she was using to rinse it.

Her heart lurched as their eyes met.

'You should be wearing a coat,' she told him without even offering a 'hello', refusing to meet his eye. 'It's bucketing down out there.'

'A bit of rainwater never hurt anyone.

Besides, I only ran from the car.'

'What are you doing here anyway?' She ran a cloth over the sink, polishing the white porcelain to perfection, giving it far more attention than the simple task required.

'Bonnie, have I done something to upset you?' His expression was puzzled.

Shocked by the unexpectedly direct question, her attention snapped up to him, the forgotten cloth dropping from her nerveless fingers.

'No.' The denial rang hollow.

He took a tentative step towards her.

'You haven't been answering my calls.'

She shrugged.

Maintaining eye contact, he took a step closer.

'Or replying to my messages.'

She sighed. How did she articulate her feelings that there was no point in any further contact when there was no future for them?

Until she had spoken to Ailsa and realised beyond doubt that there was no hope, she hadn't even known she had wanted a future with him.

But her reaction today, the way she was trembling, the fact her heart was hurting, proved beyond doubt that she was falling in love with him.

'It's best we don't see each other again.' She hadn't planned to say it, but now the words were out she knew it was the only way.

The colour drained from his face. For a moment she fancied he was as upset as she was by the prospect.

But then she quickly reminded herself that this was what he wanted. The list was his doing. He was the one who had decided that she wasn't right for him.

'You can't mean that.' His jaw clenched, and he ran rough fingers through his hair in a desperate gesture.

She nearly wavered then.

Nearly.

But even if he had been interested in pursuing a future with someone like her, the brutal truth was that he wasn't right for her, either.

She had plans. Big plans. And they didn't include a man to tie her down.

'I'm sorry, Alistair. I know there's an attraction between us, but we both know it won't work out. And if we keep dancing around the issue, one or both of use will get seriously hurt.'

'But . . . '

'You know it, too,' she insisted. 'I know about your list.'

'Ailsa! I knew I should never have told her!'

'Don't blame her. She did me a favour telling me about it. It was just the wake-up call I needed.'

'Bonnie, I've made a mess of things. I'm sorry.'

She shook her head.

'No. You've merely pointed out what was blatantly obvious. And you did that yesterday. Ailsa's visit merely drove the message home.'

His shoulders slumped.

'We could make it work.' He didn't sound convinced.

She sighed — wishing what he said was true.

'Tell me honestly, Alistair, is there a single item on that list that I meet?'

She held her breath and counted the seconds. He didn't speak.

She suddenly felt incredibly sad, just as though she had lost something of great value.

And she had.

'I didn't think so,' she said, making it easy for him in the end.

'The list was never meant to be real,' he said, realising now that was true, whatever he had said to Ailsa at the time. 'It was only a list of thoughts, ideas.'

'Goodbye, Alistair. I'll be leaving town eventually in any case, but I hope until then when we meet we can treat each other as friends.'

The fight left him then. She could see it in his eyes.

He gave a short nod.

'If that's what you want.'

And he left. Just like that, back out

into the rain that was beating down relentlessly, leaving Bonnie to worry that she had made the biggest mistake of her life.

★　★　★

Alistair was only mildly aware of the rain pelting on to his face as he made his way back to his Land Rover.

Ailsa just had to go and mention that list. Though much as he wanted to blame his sister, he knew the fault sat with nobody but himself.

Jess was sitting patiently in the passenger seat and looked up at him with adoring brown eyes as he collapsed into the driver's seat.

'I blew it, Jess,' he told the dog who had been waiting patiently for him on the passenger seat. 'The only woman who ever set foot in Shonasbrae that I might have had a future with and she doesn't want to know me.'

Jess nuzzled closer and gave a rough lick at the rain on his face.

Despite the misery in his heart, Alistair smiled. At least the dog loved him.

'Come on, girl,' he said gruffly as he started the engine, 'let's go home.'

Though the prospect didn't have its usual effect. What was the point in working so hard to make the place into a haven for a family he was unlikely never to have?

Maybe his parents had the right idea, giving it all up to travel all over the world.

For the first time ever in his life, he considered a future away from the farm. If he sold up, he would have the funds to go anywhere.

He could even go to the city. Maybe take up that engineering course he'd forgone in the farm's favour when he was a teenager.

And then it hit him in a blinding flash. He could follow Bonnie back to the city. Go with her. Marry her. Become a city boy and make a new life for himself.

His heart soared as he realised the possibility of that new vision.

He waited for the dread that hit him whenever he thought about selling the farm, but it didn't come.

Bonnie was worth it.

He was willing to give up on his beloved farm for her. And he would do it gladly.

He smiled as he stopped the car right there and then, half way up the road to the farmhouse and found himself outside the barn.

Now he'd made his decision, he couldn't wait a moment longer.

He dug out his mobile from his pocket. But before he could dial, something caught his eye.

His assurances to Bonnie yesterday that the river hadn't burst its banks in 80 years rang hollow as he saw the fast rushing water edging ever closer.

At least the animals were all well out of harm's way. But he still didn't like the look of this. He might have made the decision to walk away, but he still wanted to leave a thriving business.

The thought of everything he'd worked for being washed away by the raging river didn't sit well with him.

'We're going to have to move that stuff out of the barn,' he told the dog. And, instead of phoning Bonnie as he'd planned, he rang his farmhand's number.

'Hi, Hugh,' he said when the call was answered. 'I know it's your afternoon off, but I need your help. And can you bring Zac with you?'

★　★　★

Bonnie was aware of a fuss outside the salon. People were gathering in the street, despite the heavy rain, cars and vans driving past at as fast a speed as the weather would allow.

In the city, she wouldn't have given it a second thought — crowds of people on the pavement and busy traffic were a given.

But here, with the slower pace of life,

it seemed to signal that something serious was the matter. Given the fact she knew a number of the collected people, she grabbed her waterproof jacket and went to join them.

'What's going on?' she asked Zac.

'Dad's co-ordinating a mercy mission up to Alistair's farm.'

Bonnie felt her mouth moving, was aware of a croaking sound as she tried to speak. What had happened to Alistair? She needed to know, but the words wouldn't form on her lips.

'He phoned Dad a few minutes ago,' Zac supplied, obviously picking up on Bonnie's panic. 'He needs help. It looks as though the river will burst its bank at any moment and he's worried about the barn.'

Bonnie was aghast as she thought of all the beautiful wedding furniture and accessories he'd bought. The tables, the chairs, the coverings and linens, the crockery, the silverware, the crystal, the beautiful, beautiful things that would make a wedding so perfect for a bride and groom.

'Let me get my coat,' she said, running back into the salon. 'I'm coming with you.'

Zac took for ever to reach the farm.

Bonnie wanted to shout at him to hurry up, but she knew the lad was doing his best — driving carefully in very difficult conditions. Bonnie knew, though that there was no time to waste. The river had looked fit to bursting yesterday — the relentless rain since then would surely see it overflowing sooner rather than later.

By the time they arrived, operation save Alistair's barn was in full swing.

Bonnie leaped from Zac's car and ran straight into Alistair.

Literally.

Careered into his unmoveable chest.

'Steady,' he said as his hands came up to her arms to stop her falling.

She looked up at him and, for a moment, the rain, and the emergency, and the other mercy dashers didn't exist.

It was just the two of them and the madness all around them wasn't even on the periphery of her awareness.

'What are you doing here?' he asked eventually.

'I heard you needed help.'

Despite all his current problems, he smiled.

She couldn't believe it. And she believed it even less when her heart lurched and she felt her own lips curve into an answering grin.

'What do you need me to do?'

In an echo of what had happened yesterday, he took her hand and led her into the barn. The water, mercifully, hadn't reached the inside. Not yet at least.

'We need to move as much as we can on to a higher level.'

'I'll get a human chain organised up to the loft,' she suggested and let go of his hand to go and persuade the helpers away from the state of chaos they were currently in and into some sort of organised and cohesive unit.

Knowing Bonnie was inside keeping an eye on things meant Alistair was free to go back out into the rain and help with the sandbags.

They had been Hugh's idea. Alistair didn't know where he had sourced them from, but he was immediately grateful. They built a barricade that would give the interior of the barn the chance of protection, if the worst happened and the banks of the river burst.

They worked well as a team. Hugh had gathered the local men, the other farmers, the local businessmen, most of whom Alistair had known since he was a child.

Every time there was an emergency, they gathered round to help. Just as they were doing now, for him.

It suddenly occurred to him that, if he managed to persuade Bonnie to marry him, if they moved away, if he followed her dream alongside her, then this might be the last time he would work with these people in this way.

He allowed that to sink in.

It wasn't something he wanted, but the thought of losing Bonnie was worse.

He knew then that Bonnie was the right option.

They were putting the last sandbag into place, the noise of the river and of the rain too high to allow for idle chatter, but Zac came over and tapped his shoulder.

Alistair glanced round at whatever Zac was trying to draw his attention to.

Jess was at the water's edge, staring intently into the water.

'Looks like she's seen something,' Zac called out above the noise.

Most likely it was debris from further upstream making its way down water, but he needed to call his dog back from the edge and the dangers it represented.

'Jess,' he called gruffly.

The dog gave a yelp of acknowledgement but didn't move. She didn't even look up. Under normal circumstances she would never disregard a command from Alistair. But these were not normal circumstances and his good girl had picked up on the stress of the situation.

'Jess,' he called again, and gave the command that should have brought her to heel. Instead she stepped tentatively towards the fast-flowing water, giving a little bark as she went.

Alistair didn't hesitate. He leaped towards her, missing his step on the slippery stones on the bank and, before he knew it, the icy water was closing in around him.

He was aware of his head hitting against something solid, and everything went dark.

Husband Material

'Typical Alistair.' It was Ailsa's voice. Alistair could hear it from far away.

'Causing havoc,' his sister continued, 'then retiring to a comfortable bed to rest while everyone else tidies his farm.'

He grimaced, keeping his eyes tightly closed. He had a headache. All he wanted to do was lie still and be quiet.

'Do be quiet, Ailsa,' he mumbled. 'Some of us are trying to sleep.'

Instead of Ailsa arguing, he heard a soft sigh at his side. He knew instinctively who the third person in the room was, and forced his eyes open.

Bonnie.

He smiled — even though it hurt.

'Hi.'

Her smile was all the reward he needed for his effort, and he forced himself to concentrate. He didn't want to go back to sleep and miss a moment

235

of time that he could be spending in her company.

Hospital. It seemed he was in hospital. Leaning back against brilliant starched pillows — he could see the linen in the periphery of his vision. The stark whiteness of the room hurt his eyes, but the vision of Bonnie made him reluctant to close them, in case she disappeared.

A gnawing anxiety made his stomach contract and put his senses on red alert. Despite Bonnie's presence, he frowned, trying to remember . . .

'You gave us a fright,' Bonnie said.

Gave them a fright . . . ? How?

'Next time you decide to go for a swim, Alistair, try to find somewhere a bit safer — and don't go in fully clothed. I'm going to find your doctor and let her know you're awake.'

Go for a swim? He could tell from his sister's tone that she was being sarcastic, something Ailsa always did when she was worried. But why would she be worried?

236

And why was Bonnie at his bedside? Come to think of it, why was he in hospital?

Bonnie reached out and took his hand. He was glad. Her touch was warm and familiar and made him feel safe.

'How are you feeling?'

'I guess I'll live.'

A shadow crossed her face and he knew he shouldn't joke about such things. Not when he still wasn't sure why he was here.

And then he remembered.

'Jess.' He struggled to sit up, but Bonnie pushed him back against the pillows with gentle hands on his shoulders.

He could smell her perfume — the same scent he'd first noticed on the first day they'd met, when she'd sat beside him in the tractor.

'Jess is fine,' Bonnie assured him. 'She was fretting as we all fussed over you and waited for the paramedics to arrive. Hugh took her back to the farmhouse and promised to sort out her food.'

'I was trying to get to her.' He remembered. 'She was too close to the water.'

'As were you.' Bonnie's tone was suddenly stern. 'What were you thinking of, Alistair?'

'I wasn't,' he confessed. 'It seemed as though Jess might be swept away at any second . . . '

'When in actual fact it was you that was swept off your feet . . . '

He shrugged. It was coming back to him slowly.

'I lost my footing. Fell into the water. And hit my head on something.'

'A large rock on the riverbank,' Bonnie told him. 'Zac grabbed you before you could be washed away. I was just coming out of the barn to let you know everything was in hand, and saw it happen. Honestly, if that boy hadn't moved so fast . . . ' She shuddered in obvious horror.

'What's happening with the barn?'

'It's all good. The last I heard they think the water's receding. But you need to get those permanent flood defences in place before you do any more work on the barn or bring any more furniture in. Trying to move it all in a panic is no good for anyone's nerves.'

He nodded and winced as his head rewarded him with a dull thumping pain.

★   ★   ★

Bonnie was sick with relief that Alistair was alive and talking. She had been so worried when he had been knocked out by his fall. And sitting here beside him, she had begun to think he might never wake up.

Even when he had, he'd seemed confused for a while, but now he was conversing rationally. She began to believe he would be OK.

The past hour had been the worst of her life. And if she had ever fancied she could hide her feelings for Alistair, it was evident it wasn't true when she had cried with horror at his plight, refused to leave his side, and demanded to be allowed to accompany him in the ambulance.

Now he was so obviously OK, she was feeling more than a little foolish.

Ailsa arrived back then, with Alistair's doctor. Bonnie took the opportunity to let go of Alistair's hand and pick up her coat from where it lay on the back of her chair.

'You're not going?' He sounded alarmed. She almost relented, but she knew this was for the best.

'The doctor will need to examine you in peace.' She smiled, glanced up at Ailsa and the doctor and the nods she received from both confirmed this. 'And I need to get back to my salon.'

He gave a nod and winced.

'Take it easy,' she told him and leaned over to brush her lips against his cheek. Then she looked across at Ailsa. 'Let me know how he is.'

'I'll ring you later,' Ailsa promised.

Bonnie knew she was only opening a whole new jar of heartache for herself, asking Ailsa to keep in touch. She knew she should walk away, cut all ties, for her own peace of mind. But she had to know for sure he was OK.

If she'd had any doubt at all of her feelings for Alistair, her reaction when she saw him fall confirmed her wildest fear. She had fallen head over heels for him. The man who was only interested in marrying a woman of the type that wasn't her.

And for all that she desperately wanted to be, she knew she could never be the woman he needed or wanted. She was too focused on her own career for that.

* * *

It was with a heavy heart that she opened up the salon that afternoon.

Lianne was the first person through the door.

'What's this I hear about Alistair?' she asked. 'I saw Hugh and Zac out on the street just now. They'd said he'd had an accident.'

Bonnie nodded and gave her a brief summary of what had happened.

'He seemed OK when I left, but Ailsa's promised to let me know how he is.'

Lianne was silent for a moment, seeming to be mulling something over.

'You didn't want to stay with him yourself?'

'Well, of course. But it wouldn't have been appropriate.'

Lianne didn't look convinced.

'I think he'd have liked you to be there.'

'No,' Bonnie said sadly, realising how much the truth hurt. 'I really don't think he would.'

Bonnie's mobile buzzed to life on the counter, and she rushed over to pick it up. When she saw who was calling, her fingers trembled in her haste to press the button.

'Ailsa, how is he?'

Ailsa laughed softly down the line.

'Fine. He's fine. And asking when you might visit.'

* * *

With a clean bill of health, Alistair sighed, alone with Jess in his farmhouse when he knew Bonnie belonged with him.

He was going to have to make things right with her. And he was going to start with his blasted list. Written in haste, repented at leisure. And then some.

He took the crumpled scrap of paper out of the dresser drawer. His glance rested ruefully on the scrawl of his own handwriting. He'd thought, when he'd written it, that this list had held the answer to everything.

Then he'd met Bonnie.

Jaw clenched, he slowly ripped the list into two, the sound of paper tearing more satisfying than it should have been. Then he ripped it again. And again. And didn't stop until tiny pieces of confetti covered the floor.

The weight of that task lifted, he knew the most important job was still to come. Convincing Bonnie wasn't going to be easy.

He'd hoped that she might have forgiven him when she turned up at the barn to help. And when she'd been sitting at his bedside at the hospital when he'd woken up. Then she had disappeared, and he hadn't heard a word from her since.

Surely she cared? Why would she have bothered to come up to the farm to help him out, otherwise? And why would she have gone with him in the ambulance, waiting until he'd woken up, if it didn't mean she had feelings for him?

It was that belief that had him arriving at the salon on a dull, but remarkably not rainy, afternoon.

She was on the phone when he walked in, pen in hand, taking a booking for a cut and blow dry.

She looked up when he came in. Their eyes locked, and her smile had his heart racing madly against his chest.

'That's great. I'll see you tomorrow at ten,' she told the customer, maintaining eye contact with Alistair the whole time. 'Goodbye for now.'

'Are you going to write that booking down, before you forget?' he asked, when she still hadn't moved after a few minutes.

She nodded, turned the page of her diary, and scribbled the booking in.

'How are you?' she asked, her attention back on him.

He shrugged, then grinned.

'Yeah, good, thanks.'

'I'm very pleased to hear it.'

He wished he had the words that would make things right between them. Maybe he should have rehearsed a speech. But he hadn't been able to wait — now he'd made up his mind, he didn't want to waste another second of his life without her.

'I'm sorry,' he said, 'about that whole wife list thing.'

She shrugged a slender shoulder.

'None of my business how you choose to find a wife, Alistair.'

He took a step closer.

'But it is. Your business, I mean. Very much so.'

She shook her head.

'I'm glad you made me see that we're not compatible. That we want different things out of life.'

He frowned. What if he was wrong? What if she didn't want him, after all?

'What do you want, Bonnie?' he forced himself to ask, even though he was frightened to hear her answer in case it wasn't the one he wanted.

She smiled. A rather sad smile that tore at his heart. He wanted to gather her up into his arms and never let her go.

'The same as everyone else, I guess. To be happy.'

'Do you think I could make you happy?' He held his breath as he waited for her to respond.

'Yes,' she said at last. 'Yes, even if it meant rethinking my plans and staying in Shonasbrae, you could. But I know I wouldn't make you happy.'

'You'd be willing to stay in Shonasbrae for me?'

'In a heartbeat.'

He gave into temptation then and stepped closer to bring his arms around her. He felt tentative arms go about his waist, her head on his shoulder . . .

'But I'm not farmer's wife material. I may not be any kind of wife material. Before meeting you, settling down wasn't even on my list of priorities.'

He kissed the top of her hair and she lifted her head to look up at him, before brushing her lips against his.

'I never thought I'd be a beautician's husband material, but I really think we can make it work,' he told her fiercely.

She smiled then. And took his breath away. He knew in that instant that he would do anything he could to make her happy. Because that's what you did when you loved someone as much as he loved Bonnie.

Really he hadn't stood a chance from the moment he'd first met her. Even if his head had resisted to the last, his heart had known all along exactly what it wanted.

We do hope that you have enjoyed reading this large print book.

Did you know that all of our titles are available for purchase?

We publish a wide range of high quality large print books including:
Romances, Mysteries, Classics
General Fiction
Non Fiction and Westerns

Special interest titles available in large print are:
The Little Oxford Dictionary
Music Book, Song Book
Hymn Book, Service Book

Also available from us courtesy of Oxford University Press:
Young Readers' Dictionary
(large print edition)
Young Readers' Thesaurus
(large print edition)

For further information or a free brochure, please contact us at:
Ulverscroft Large Print Books Ltd.,
The Green, Bradgate Road, Anstey,
Leicester, LE7 7FU, England.
Tel: (00 44) **0116 236 4325**
Fax: (00 44) **0116 234 0205**

SAVING ALICE

Gina Hollands

Naomi Graham is the best family lawyer in the country. But beneath her professional demeanour lies a broken heart. When the man who caused that heartache — billionaire ex-husband Toren Stirling — returns to her life after a ten-year absence, Naomi doesn't want to know. Their painful struggle to start a family tore their relationship apart, so when Toren reveals that he has a young daughter, Alice, it comes as a shocking blow. Not only that, but he's now fighting a custody battle — and needs Naomi's legal expertise to help him win.